RED EYES AND TIRED LUNGS

AN ANTHOLOGY OF WILDFIRE
EDITED BY ASHA JADE GOODWIN

Winter Jewel Publishing

For more information on previous, current, or future projects, please visit winterjewelpublishing.ca

Book Cover design by Asha Jade Goodwin

Cover Art by Lumitar (Oksana Drozd) via Deposit Photos

First edition 2024

ISBN: 978-1-7381603-2-7 (Hardcover)
ISBN: 978-1-7381603-0-3 (Paperback)
ISBN: 978-1-7381603-1-0 (eBook)

CONTENTS

Introduction   1

Caution   5
By Jaki Sawyer

Evacuation Orders Issued   9
By Raegan Cote

Breaking News   13
by Morgan Allie Graylin

Rage   19
By Heather Bonin MacIntosh

What Is Worth Protecting?   23
Interview with Jen Herkes

Anatomy of a Wildfire   31
by Rod Raglin

Flax Finds A Flameling   37
By Asha Jade Goodwin

One breath of hot, toxic gases can fatally burn a   55
firefighter's lungs and airway.
by Tyree Corfe

Change Takes Time   59
By Kilmeny MacMichael

Smoke and Tears   81
By Lesley Hebert

Smoke Hurts   85
by Hilma Sinkinson

Into the Great Unknown   97
by Asha Jade Goodwin

Flamebound   103
By Topper Sundquist

Fire Season   121
By Michele Rule

Perceptions of Desire   125
By Asha Jade Goodwin

West Kelowna Burns   131
By Jaki Sawyer

Return   135
by Alexander Robertson

Unrelenting   141
By Raegan Cote

Frogging Hour   145
By Em Van Moore

Haikus From A Midnight Morning   157
by Asha Jade Goodwin

They Called Us Monsters   161
by Drea Laj

August 17, 2023   169
By Rod Raglin

Burning Eyes   173
By Payne Haynes

Smoke Choked Skies   179
By Asha Jade Goodwin

What World Is This?   183
by Cherie Hanson

Ten little Nomads   189
by Lily Autumn West

Sugar Juice   193
By Lily Autumn West

The Earth is Breaking Up with Me   199
By Cherie Hanson

Beast   203
By Cassidy Muir

Something Good   207
By Kilmeny MacMichael

Hearts Aflame   213
By Jonathan Riggs

Vancouver Future   229
By Anneliese Schultz

Parched   233

By Asha Jade Goodwin

Long Wave   243

By Kilmeny MacMichael and Asha Jade Goodwin

All The Help We Can Get   247

By Asha Jade Goodwin

Acknowledgements   281

Biographies   284

INTRODUCTION

In the summer of 2023, the Donnie Creek Wildfire spread over 600,000 hectares – a wildfire larger than the entire province of PEI. The fire was northeast of Prince George, and it, as well as many other wildfires that blazed across Northern BC, poured smothering smoke into the city and across the province. For weeks we squinted through orange haze, coughing until our chests ached, watching bears attack our garbage cans, hardly daring to spend more than a moment outdoors except for the rare hours a clear breeze blew by and momentarily bestowed blue skies. What do you do when you can barely breathe the air outside?

This anthology started as the title, said to myself as I walked to my car one smoky afternoon. *I've got red eyes and tired lungs,* I thought, as I waded through the choking air. The sentence seemed to bounce around my head, wanting to burst out of me – in a poem, or a story, I wasn't sure. I played around with it, rolled it, squished it, but it wasn't forming into anything significant, nothing more than a few scattered lines. It wanted to be something, but it wasn't responding to my hands just yet. However, a writer friend asked for a prompt, I shared it with them, and the next thing I knew they had written an entire poem. I loved it, but I also felt like we weren't done. That phrase – *Red Eyes and Tired Lungs* – begged to be so much more.

The same day I came up with the idea of turning it into an anthology, I shared it with the rest of my writer group. I'd always wanted to do a project with local writers but had struggled to find a topic worthy of the endeavor and did not feel like I had the experience to start such an undertaking. However, once that line existed, the rest was set in motion and I knew I had to see this all the way through.

And so the next few months were spent reading, writing, reviewing, and editing stories and poems from writers near and far. So many writers seized upon the heart of the anthology and poured themselves into it, even while they were being affected by the smoke and wildfires.

What does it mean, "An Anthology of Wildfire"? The greatest challenge to creating this anthology was making sure we tackled the theme from as many angles as possible. Wildfire is dynamic, both a destructive force as well as a part of the cycle of renewal. We can't have one without the other, and only talking about the bad *or* the potential good would be doing a disservice to everyone who has felt the effects of either. If this anthology was only about happily burning old, dry tinder and planting in the newly fertile soil, that wouldn't be very honest, would it? Conversely, only talking about the loss of homes, of lives, would be incredibly depressing – and while I love the emotional depth of a good tragedy, that wouldn't be telling the full story either. We need all of the stories, all of the perspectives, all of the ups and downs that come with something so terrifying and yet also necessary. Why is fire necessary? It returns nutrients to the soil, gives space for new growth, and some trees –

Jack and Lodgepole Pine, for example – can only release their seeds through the heat of fire. Wildfire is, clearly, multi-faceted, and so should our writing about it be as well.

In this anthology you will find a collection of poems and stories by twenty one different authors, inspired by and in response to the wildfires that have ravaged our province and across Canada. Living in British Columbia, these wildfire-filled summer seasons have left us no strangers to having red eyes and tired lungs, and through these poems and stories readers will be able to take a walk through our experiences and imaginations. Over the course of this endeavor that has spanned three seasons – and has almost brought us back to fire season once more – I've heard from so many voices and met so many amazing authors. I've ignited my own passion for editing, and further fanned the flames of my love for writing. From this work, thirty-five brand new pieces are presented to the world to showcase the talent and heart of the authors who wrote them.

Thank you for supporting an independent publisher!

CAUTION

By Jaki Sawyer

Baked crisp
Steep parched slopes
Tilted deadfall
Brittle pine and fir
Like dark candles
Desiccated branches
Arranged like kindling
The whole forest
Ready for a spark

Evacuation Orders Issued

By Raegan Cote

Evacuation orders issued,
expanded as B.C's wildfire threat refuses to subside
- CBCNews headline, Sept. 17, 2023

I, the threat.

   take 100 years of firefighting — fighting me — and I
will give you one summer
to remember.

leave fire scars across lands
forgotten by government funding.
inch under ground,
& watch them

dig   dig   dig

till autumn
traps embers
below.

pass sparrow
pass   black bear & grizzly
elk   deer   fox
oh worm
     oh mosses
          oh cell tower
I blaze on, inferno

moving
four five six   km/hour

so they say.

creep over live vegetation,
                              dead vegetation,
this branch, this non-branch, this soot
I unravel.

& just imagine—
I began only a spark.

BREAKING NEWS

BY MORGAN ALLIE GRAYLIN

The little red dot blinks.

I keep scrolling, keep reading, keep hoping they'll tell me what the sky outside can't.

I look again, past the water-spotted window to the orange smoky haze; nothing new there. Still, the little red dot blinks. There's breaking news – that blinking red dot tells me so – but nothing's breaking. Not here. Not yet.

There's a rustle of blankets from the bedroom. Nothing new there either; Jake is still sleeping even though I've tried to wake him twice already. He should be up, watching the sky, watching the little red dot blink. I fiddle absently with the keys in my sweater pocket, his lighter and the handful of bobby pins living there pinging against each other.

The bed creaks and then the floorboards follow as he staggers into the kitchen.

"They say we should know today which way it's going," I tell him, turning my phone in my hands.

He's in the fridge, squinting against the light. "Are we out of milk?"

"I read online that we should fill up our cans with water. Might need to take a run to the transfer station to empty them, though."

He's jostling the contents of the fridge. "I swear we still had a bag left."

"I packed some stuff in your gym duffel. You can check if there's anything else you want to add to it?"

"I'll stop at the store and grab some when I go to Trevor's later, I guess," he says, pouring a cup of coffee from the machine before turning back to the bedroom, the liquid sloshing against the side of his mug with each unsteady step until he sets it on the nightstand and falls back into bed.

I look back down at my phone. The little red dot blinks.

Breaking news.

It's breaking and it's blinking and all I see is red.

My footsteps are swift as they cross the space between us, my hands steady as they slam the window upwards and the thick, sour, smoke-heavy air pours in.

He jumps up, pushing past me as he slams the window closed again, coughing and sputtering as he does. "What the fuck is wrong with you?"

"What's not wrong, Jake? I'm just trying to be prepared and you won't even talk about it–"

"I'm sick of talking about the fire, Kels! I'm sick of hearing you fucking talk about the fire. I'm done. I'm done talking about the goddamn fire." He's pulling on his pants.

"You don't get to just check out and be done. You don't think I'm tired of talking about the fire? Someone has to be the grownup here, someone has to–"

"Fine," he snaps, reaching for the window, ripping it back open with a force that rattles the frame and springs the screen free. "You want the window open? Fine! There's your open window."

He turns, pulling his shirt over his head as he goes, an unlit cigarette dangling precariously from the corner of his mouth as he escapes out of the bedroom and through the kitchen, towards the side door. I follow, and he's pulling on his boots.

"Where are you going? You can't just leave–"

He curses under his breath, but the squealing and slam of the screen door is his only answer.

The truck at the end of the drive roars to life, and it's rumbling away, and I can feel it in my chest long after he's gone down the road. I feel it rumbling as I walk back to the bedroom, back to the open window, back to our bed. I feel it rumbling as tears wet my cheeks and my chest heaves and the sobs that escape join the rolling, rattling chorus.

I cry. The little red dot blinks and the air is so pungent and heavy and I can taste it on the tears that wet my lips and I cry. I cry until my eyes are red and my lungs are tired, until there are no more tears and the rumbling has rolled away.

Still, the little red dot blinks because it's breaking news; it's never done. But this – here – isn't breaking news.

Creaky floorboards, the squealing door, the final heavy slam that gives way to rustling leaves and the faraway rhythmic thumping of helicopters somewhere that's not here.

The grass has been cut so short it's patchy and scratches against my bare feet as I trek around the side of the house towards the hose; past the trees whose branches have been trimmed and severed so severely on the house-facing side they'll likely never recover; past the garbage cans, lids closed, trash and cleared yard waste stashed out of sight, out of mind. A small branch lies beside them, its leaves brown and dry. Had he chucked it there, missed the bin and simply considered it close enough? Was it? I pick it up as I go.

The nozzle drips, ever so slightly, from where it hangs on the hook, pinging against the tangled mess of rubber hose on the ground beneath it, wound and unwound and discarded. I step over it, turning the water valve.

The drip stops.

I'm standing beneath the bedroom window now – our bedroom window – and his lighter's no longer in my pocket and the branch in my hand is no longer dry; it's burning, fast and hot and smoky, and it's sailing through the open window.

I never wanted the window open.

My phone lights up in my hand and the little red dot is still blinking. Something's breaking somewhere out there, but nothing here is breaking; it's already broken.

We'll blame the open window.

RAGE

By Heather Bonin MacIntosh

Alder Ash anchors the air

Bitter Cherry Branches bubble and burn

Cedar Charred conifers crumble and choke out

Dogwood Dreams of downpours, and we despair.

Engelmann Spruce Embers on easterlies, and

Fir Floaters fan the forest fury

Green Alder Glowing, gloaming, gone.

Hemlock Heat hurls itself at homes and haunts highways.

Ironwood Injury impels us to search for

Jack Pine Justice. Just. Or not.

Kenai Birch Knocked off course,

Lodgepole Lifting a lament of

Mountain Maple Misery and mourning.

Narrowleaf Cottonwood Nests necessary for

Oak Owls and orioles, obliterated.

Poplar Perches perish as

Queen Anne's Lace Quails quiet in

Red Elderberry Retreat along razed ranges, their

Scarlet Hawthorn Sybil songs subdued.

Trembling Aspen Thickets are terrorized by

Umbrella Pine Underbrush under fire in a

Violet Verbena Valley of vermillion.

White Ash Wretched and wrecked,

X-hybrids X-ed from existence, and yet

Yew Yearn for exotic zones, far from a

Zebrawood Zenith of flame.

Eyes red, lungs tired, as the world rages. Or not.

What is Worth Protecting?

Interview with Jen Herkes

I've been working since 2020 on a Wildfire Risk Assessment Project. My work takes me to the Yukon, where I work with two First Nations – Carcross/Tagish First Nation, and Kwanlin Dun First Nation. My time with them is spent gathering traditional knowledge and research.

With those particular nations, or at least where I was studying, they did not specifically manage the land with fire. I've been involved peripherally with some other nations where they did – they would burn areas specifically for regeneration to maintain meadows, so that specific animals and plants will grow back. Our research found that these Nations didn't do cultural or prescribed burning in this area, but that fire was a very respected feature on the land. They lived far more nomadically, so they moved around a lot more, following the animals, and they didn't have a permanent residence. When we talked to people and asked them questions like "How did you deal with wildfires in the past? What did you do if there was a wildfire?" They told us "You'd just move out of its way."

In a lot of the traditional stories that I read, fire represents something like a passageway, a device, that people could communicate across the spiritual plane with. There are a lot of old stories about animals teaching people or animals giving people knowledge; in most of those stories, the animals appear as humans. Afterwards, you find out that it was perhaps a Grizzly Bear who was there, or another animal. In most of those stories they meet across a fire, often a campfire, but the main themes are always that you're sitting on the opposite side of the fire and then once the fire burns down, that's when you understand who you are actually talking to. The stories show fire as a way of life, connecting people to that other spiritual dimension.

We researched and learned about the traditional knowledge, and then came up with a final summary report of our findings. Next, we worked with a fire and forest ecologist who does a lot of work on Vancouver Island. He was working to develop a forest risk assessment, using a bunch of information such as lightning strikes, weather patterns, forest type, fuel (what type of fuel there is for the fire to consume), how old is the forest, and how much fuel there would be to burn. He then uses all that information to figure out what are the chances of a fire happening in an area, and if a fire were to start, what kind of damage could it do. This information is also based on wind and other factors. With the assessment he created, we did some community engagement and we talked to the citizens about what values are important. The primary value is often people's property and homes. Life and homes are basically the two top priorities. That's why we saw in BC this year that the majority of efforts were put towards fires near Kelowna and other cities, while the other fires further out were just left to burn. It was more important to protect those people and their houses.

Still, we wanted to understand more beyond those two priorities – life and home – what else on the land is worth protecting. In the area where I was working, that was caribou, land use – which we interpreted as cabins and camps – and salmon. These were the main values other than people's homes. Then we take that first layer that the forest ecologist developed that asks, "What are the chances of there being a fire?" Next, the Nations take that information and look at the layer of "What are their values?" and they look for the spots where it is the most overlapping.

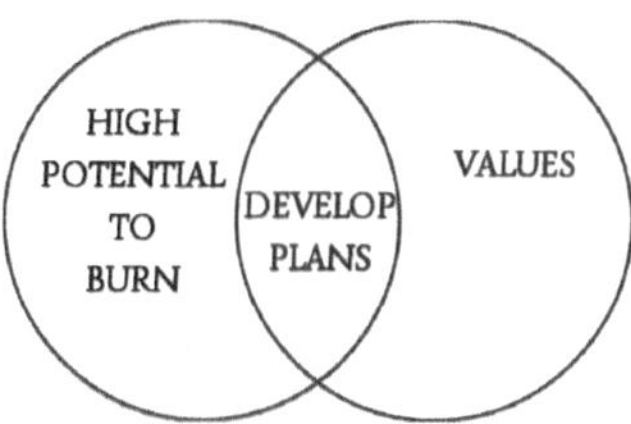

Those are the areas that we want to develop plans to protect. If we then know an area is important because of these values and it also has a high potential to burn down, how do we fix that? The two main ways recommended were doing prescribed burning and fire breaks.

Prescribed burning is burning off certain areas that have high fuel loads; high potential to keep a fire going and push it along. The other option, fire breaks, is to cut and clear out all the fuel that might be on the ground. Evergreen trees often need to be cleared out because they burn hotter than the deciduous trees.

At this point in the project, we've got all these tools available to us to develop a plan and then the plan will go to the communities for implementation. "Here's what the experts say you should do," but a lot of the recommendations can be unrealistic. For example, one of the recommendations is to make fire breaks by going in and cutting down all of the evergreen trees along the highways, but make a break of about 100 metres on each side of the highway. Which is a wide area, and people enjoy the way that the wilderness looks. Cutting all of that down – I just don't know if they're going to get community buy in for that. It's interesting to consider – this could stop the fire from destroying a bunch of values, including houses, but people aren't willing to give up that aesthetic. Another factor to consider is it would impact the environment and habitats of animals. If you take out all the evergreen, now there's going to be wild animals that will be displaced or not able to live in that area anymore.

It's an interesting trade-off, and like you mentioned, it seems that we have had a shift in culture but it's only to some extent. We are willing to invest in some changes but not if it affects us too much. Otherwise, we are willing to take the risk almost without a lot of actual thought put into what will happen.

So that is part of what I've been working on. It's interesting because this last summer, one of my friend's camps burnt down. They think somebody left a campfire going. It burned down all their cabins and then it caused this huge fire that started moving up the lake. BC wildfire didn't do anything about it because to them it was in the middle of nowhere and their focus was on the Kelowna area this year because we have people's houses being threatened by fire, versus this situation. It wasn't endangering communities directly, although it was endangering some cabins. There were a few cabins that set up their own sprinklers and took care of themselves. They were fine, but we got to a point where the fire was starting to get really close to one of the Heritage sites that we know of that is a fairly important site for one of the Nations' families. It was interesting because we sent a letter to BC Wildfire and told them, "Hey, no one has contacted us, because the Nation is in the Yukon although their territory also goes into BC. I'm just wondering what's going on with this fire. We do have some cultural resources and some heritage resources that are potentially at risk if it continues to move and burn freely." BC Wildfires were really good, and they responded within a day of getting the letter. They flew Charlie out, the guy whose family area was at risk, and an archeologist to go and take a look at things and come up with a plan. But they explained that they only had one pump and some hoses that they could use to help with. And Charlie, a Carcross/Tagish Elder, explained that the cabins are not what we are worried about. It's the trees, the environment, the land – that's what we are afraid of losing. We should have fought this fire when it was just the cabin's burning at the end of the lake because then there would have been loss, but not as much lost.

That has been my fire experience in the last couple of years.

Interview with Jen Herkes occurred on December 28th, 2023. Transcribed and edited with approval by Asha Jade Goodwin.

Anatomy of a Wildfire

by Rod Raglin

The forest scent is spicy evergreen, stale hardwood,
aged, clean, combustible
beneath the canopy the air is stagnant, thick with
heat
everything crunches and crackles
shriveled salal, brittle windfall kindling, a carpet of
fuel decades thick
even the bugs have abandoned the golden shafts
filtering through the sagging bows.

The raven, seeking shelter from the sun-bleached sky
studies the slaked pond now a puddle
where bullfrog tadpoles flounder.

A whiff of tainted wind.

The raven lifts off without warning
an unseen buck crashes through the undergrowth
the bear abruptly abandons the huckleberries
invertebrates slither for safety or begin to burrow
below.

Survival depends on heading downslope in the right
direction
hoping the wind doesn't increase and launch
incendiary cinders, flaming precursors
that will send the burning back upon them.

Encouraged by a brisk breeze and an insatiable
appetite
the beast devours everything in its path
the forest floor inferno reaches twelve hundred
degrees Celsius
boulders crack, trees candle and explode jettisoning
flames
one hundred and fifty feet into the seared air

the maelstrom creates its own cyclone
rips out trees, sucks them into the superheated
column
hurls them like burning spears
while vortexes of twisting flame fling fiery shrapnel
with a voice like a gigantic blowtorch, the revving of
jet engines prior to take off
it exhales giant billowing plumes that create thunder,
even rain
that never reaches the ground

only the lightning
igniting more forest.
As lanky shrubs, bark flakes and tree lichens add
vertical continuity
between the blaze below and the fuels in the crowns
above
the tree tops torch, and hot wind fans the firestorm.

Longer now and longer to come
the fire season
spawns epic blazes that thwart
even the most aggressive attempts at suppression
breaching   fire   lines,   invading   interfacing
communities
destroying indiscriminately, dispassionately

Even when autumn rains and cooler weather
brings respite from choking smoke and stinging haze
the   aftermath   of   scorched   earth   creates   new
disasters:
landslides, ash-flows, flash floods, polluted water

and all the while
beneath the soothing snow
smoldering deep below the charred remains
the beast still lives waiting
for the next, hotter, wildfire season.

FLAX FINDS A FLAMELING

By Asha Jade Goodwin

All these years away from home and Flax is still terrified to step into a forest. The fear radiates from the heat of the unknown: what will happen if he finds himself back in the Unending Forest? They gave him grace to escape last time. He would not be shown mercy twice.

But he is years away from the Unending Forest, the heart of this province is on fire, and no one but him could possibly traverse those flame-soaked trees safely. The humans flit about: moaning, sobbing, ash-painted faces streaked with tears, cradling charred limbs, brushing off burnt hair. Their red-rimmed eyes are a contrast to his yellow. *Home!* they cry out to the strange little dryad who pretends he is a witch even though he is so much more. *Our home is burning.* He does not have a home anymore either, he wants to tell them, but it does not seem like an appropriate time.

"I will find the source of these flames," he tells no one in particular, curiousity always sending him where he should not go. The humans are not listening anyways. Their sobs have turned to barking coughs and they are fleeing now, down the valley, embers trailing. Flax expects the entire valley will be roaring in flames soon, and some part of him wants to sit and watch the flames pour out of the forest like a river dam breaking. The little bit inside of him that knows all the things he should not has a morbid fascination with the change fire brings. The fragment of the man he had apparently once been tells him to stay, to watch the destruction as it consumes.

Sometimes he listens to the voice. Today he does not.

The dryad steps into the burning forest, disappearing into the choking smoke. He leaves his hat and cloak behind.

Flames lick the trees with long tongues as he steps gingerly across the burning carpet. Sweat beads at his temple and he wipes it, flicking the droplets away. They sizzle as they touch the flames, but where the droplets land green sprouts bloom only to blacken and crisp in the heat. He leaves a spiky, withered trail through the underbrush.

His lungs are at this point vestigial, and he feels them stutter and stop as the smoke grows too thick to breathe through. The humans fleeing far behind would no doubt have already fallen to the flame had any tried to follow. Flax is glad he is no longer beholden to such limitations. His second life, as a dryad, has been filled with marvelous benefits. Even his inability to light a fire of his own is simply an interesting challenge to overcome as he needs.

Flax passes through the remains of houses that once littered the woods, now splintered and charred. They burn, filled with flame, fire reaching up into the sky. Red and orange, they seem to dance excitedly. Nothing but ash remains in their wake.

Take some, says the voice inside him. Charcoal can be used for many different applications, but this charcoal still burns too hot. Although Flax would heal from the burns and they would be little more than superficial injuries, he does not want to slow. He needs to continue on, find the truth of this place.

The humans had been taken unaware, the fire sprouting and spreading at wicked speeds. These are not natural born flames.

The world grows hotter still.

Flax hears it, the screech of some strange creature deep in the forest. At first, he fears it is a wild animal, some poor bear or fox or deer has been trapped and surrounded by fire. But this screech is like no earthly sound he has ever heard before, and even if it is terrified as it chokes, he does not think a regular animal could have made that sound. No, there is no ordinary creature screaming in this forest – the smart ones are fleeing, the rest are dead. The screech is more like a call, enticing, mourning. However, Flax knows that any prey would heed that howl as a warning.

And then he sees it. In the middle of an ash-blackened clearing, fire-transformed trees now soot, there is a creature – something that he has never seen before, not in this life. At first he does not even realize it is a being, because it has feathers that match the fires that are sizzling across the clearing still. It is a monster born of fire. It is a massive, winged bird, with a wingspan the size of two men, and feathers of flickering, faint flames. It has a long, beautiful neck and a hard, ashen beak. Somewhere beneath all that flame is coal-dark skin, as if the skeleton has burned away to char. And yet it seems able to fly! Looking at it, Flax knows he should feel fear. This is not a being of this world, it should not reside here, not even survive; this place is filled with life and rain – it will no doubt absolutely drown such a monster. He can imagine rain sizzling against the skin of the creature. It can never thrive in this land.

Perhaps that is why it burns the forest, Flax tells himself. He imagines the heat must feel like home to this strange animal from another world. This bird-like being had no doubt been born and bathed in flames. He imagines that the creature will find itself consumed, staying alive by the heat it makes for itself. Flax wonders if it is possible to keep the forest hot enough for it to live.

Flax steps closer and the crack of charred twigs beneath his feet draws the attention of the bird to him. He looks down, confused – he has never broken plants before with his steps. This creature has molded the very environment around it until it is unrecognizable as the place it was. This forest is now incompatible with Flax, like the rocky streets of the human-paved cities. It hurts him to tread and break these plants even though he knows they are already dead. He flicks more sweat onto them, and tiny green sprouts rise around him. *Life can still bloom, even in the most inhospitable of places.*

Here the smoke is thick but the flames, other than the ones that came from the strange fiery bird, are thin. There is not much more for it to burn. It turns towards Flax, focusing its attention on him. Its eyes are two dark coals in an unforgiving face.

It yells at Flax, the great crackling of an angry fire, and yet he can hear a word there. An impossible word, in a language he should not understand. "Who?" It screeches. "Why?" It begs. Confused, Flax stares at the bird. What is this strange being that speaks with flame? He has never possessed a gift of language – even dryads from other groves had been incomprehensible to him until he learned their words for the world. And yet this strange, impossible being from another world is able to converse with him.

"What are –" Flax pauses, trying to decide what he should ask. Both questions feel strangely aggressive towards this unknown creature, despite the destruction it caused. His thoughts drift back to the destruction and mistakes he has inadvertently caused in his life, and this gives him pause. Could he show the monster mercy he was not given? "– you doing here?"

"Free!" it caws. "New skies, blue skies, away from the unending red and scattered sands. But cold, our new home is cold, and the animals flee."

Flax wonders if his first impression has been correct about the bird, that it is trying to stay warm and that is how it lit the entire forest on fire. A name comes to him, from somewhere deep inside, from the man that had lived so long ago that he had memories of legends. *Chaoswing*, he tells Flax. A simple label for an incredible creature.

"I do not understand," says Flax, as he takes another step closer. "Where is your home?" He tries to remember what the bird said. "Your home had red skies?"

"Our home is gone, and so too are the red skies of the egg we waited in," it moans. "But we are alone. This is no home for us."

Flax wants to deny this – he knows intimately the desire for a home. He has been searching for one since the day he stepped out of the Forest. The keening longing for somewhere in the world where he can belong. Perhaps there is somewhere in this world where he can live, a place he could carve out and sculpt to be his own. He has not found it yet, but he is sure that it must exist.

But what about the chaoswing? It could not live in this place. It will grow and consume and destroy everything it touches until there is nothing left, just like it already has. It cannot remain in this place.

"Why do you not go back?" Flax asks. "To your egg." He is not sure if the egg is a literal place, or a metaphor, or something lost in translation.

"We have lost the way," it croons sadly, and then sweeps its wings. A burst of flame spreads from it. Flax has to shield his face, and he feels his arm blister and blacken in the heat. "We know not the path." It lets out a wailing screech.

Flax looks at the utter destruction that surrounds him. It is hard to imagine that such a path would be very difficult to follow. "Perhaps I can help you," he offers.

The chaoswing swivels its head and one coal-black eye regards him. "We would consume you." It is not a threat, just a fact;

the chaoswing is subject to its nature, and its nature is to light everything on fire, turning everything to cinders. "We would feast on your flesh." It seems to bark at him.

Flax is taken aback, but he recovers quickly. "I have no flesh to feast on," he tells the bird. "You hunt?"

"For our children, so they may grow as strong as us." The chaoswing turns, stretching a fiery wing, and Flax sees a few dots of spirited flame on the back of the creature. *Flamelings,* the voice inside comes unbidden. He can see there are a few of them twirling on the back of the chaoswing, flitting about as if buffeted by unseen wind. He does not bother trying to count them but notices the smallest one seems less agile than the rest. It sits by the tail, away from the rest. Flax waits patiently for the voice in his head to continue.

Flamelings do not turn if they do not consume meat, the voice tells him in its familiar, lecturing way; reciting something it once knew. *They never grow larger than a fist without flesh.* None of the flamelings are bigger than a fist, Flax notices. The smallest, the runt, is smaller than a dandelion bud.

"I would like to help you find your way back-" Flax stops, remembering that the bird has no home. He does not want to set off another wave of fire. "Back to where you were before. It is a safe place?"

The chaoswing wails anyways, and Flax has to momentarily retreat. He pats the flames out that lick at the bark on his arms. He is not sure what he can possibly say or do to make the chaoswing happy.

Does it need to be happy, though? Flax wonders if that is the wrong solution. If the chaoswing does not move on, it will cause immense destruction. Or it may die – humans are quite adept at killing. A wandering knight has no doubt been summoned already. Flax doubts a human would be able to traverse this forest – the air is too thick with smoke. They will choke and die. But if the chaoswing moves to a new place, the knight will follow, and it will kill the bird.

That is what knights do with the strange and different. They kill. Flax has experienced his own run-ins with knights in the past. It usually takes a lot to convince a knight that he is not a monster that will harm humanity, and he can speak their language. It is why there are no more dragons in the known world. It is why dryads do not stray from their Unending Forest.

This chaoswing is absolutely a creature that will harm humans. Flax does not doubt it; he is not naïve. Not anymore. But does that mean that it must die, just because it is a slave to its nature?

"If you stay in this place, humans will come for you and kill you," he tells the chaoswing.

The bird seems to bristle at the implication. "Once we worked with humans. They flew on our backs. We gave them our eggs. We had a human once. We left them in the red skies." It resettles. "Are you not a human?"

"I am not," Flax assures it.

"What are you?"

"I am still trying to figure that out." He ponders how a human can ride this creature. Will they not be a charred husk in minutes? Sweat pours off him, blooming grass beneath his feet that immediately wilts in the heat.

And then Flax notices it. The bird is *sick*. Are the flames, the scorching heat, a symptom of an infection, just like a fever is in humans? Perhaps the creature always burns, but if the flames are not always so hot, it may be possible to ride them. If a human wears thick enough clothing, at any rate.

Flax is sure of it. The chaoswing is sick. It is the only thing that makes sense to him. The strange bark he heard earlier was a cough. The heat. Even the eyes, coal-black as they are, are feverish. Flax has taken care of so many sick people and animals in his life already that he knows the symptoms across species. He is ashamed he did not recognize it quicker.

"You are sick," he tells the bird. "I can help you." He is not sure if he can. Already his mind is racing through all the animals he has ever cared for, but none are at all similar to what rests before him. Can he even make it tea? Will it drink water? Can it?

Flax has so much to think over. It is overwhelming. He sits down on a charred log. "I am not sure what you need," he admits. "Normally I give a little bit of huppade for sickness. Usually I mix it with some willow bark. Brew it in a tea. But is that what you need?"

The chaoswing does not answer. Flax looks over and notices that it has gone to sleep.

Flax takes a moment to try and figure out what exactly he is going to do for the bird. He goes through what he remembers of the different plants that he has seeds for and how they can potentially help. His first thought is to use hibernation catnip, because of its cooling effect. But as he glances over at the bird, sees the flames that flicker from it, and wonders if those flames can be fully doused. Will hibernation catnip work the same way for such a creature? If he brings down the temperature of the bird too much, like hibernation cabinet will likely do, can he kill it? It is not something he wants to risk, not yet.

There is also the issue that some plants are poisonous to different beings. He has learned over the years how vegetation that is fine or even delicious to one animal can instantly kill another. He does consider that if he accidentally kills the chaoswing, he will be solving the problem in a circumventive way, but he does not want to do that. Flax wants to make sure that he gives this creature a chance.

In the end he settles on using willow bark.

Flax begins to search for what he needs, trying to see if there is a still-alive tree nearby. It is not impossible for him to grow a new one, but he does not want to waste his seeds where they will not thrive.

It is when Flax arrives at a river that he suddenly realizes he is no longer alone. He bends over the water, watches the dirty, ashen waves rolling, thinking of how to filter the soot when he notices the reflection behind him.

"And who're you, wandering this forest? No human, I'm sure."

Flax turns and looks at the metallic visage of a knight. It reflects his own face back at him, distorted by the bend of the plating and the deep blue tint of the metal. Despite the colour, the armour itself is plain, unadorned. There are only a few scratches marring the surface. This person is short for a human, and there is a slight tremble in the arm that grips the crossbow, even though the weapon is not raised. Is the knight tired, or afraid?

"You must be sweating in there," he comments in an easy manner, still kneeling at the riverbed. He knows enough of knights to not rise quickly, to not startle them. Just what he needs, a knight getting their nose in his business. He wishes they would take off their helmet, show their face to him. His chance of survival depends on the tattoo that marks their face.

"It is a little hot," the knight admits in a feminine, young voice. Flax can see a strange film covering the mouthpiece of the helmet. It reminds him of parsh gossamer. He wonders if that is why the knight is not straining from the smoke. He does not know much of human magics; he wonders, if there is a way to breathe the smoky air, why it has not been given to all the humans. Perhaps there was not enough time. Something else bothers Flax – this knight does not seem to have a chronicler, someone to record their heroic deeds. He wonders if she is young enough that she has not earned one, or that there was not time for a second mask to be made. "Are you dangerous?" She asks. There is a slight warble in her voice. Flax shakes his head. "Did you cause this forest fire?"

"I have been trying to end it," he tells her.

She seems to accept this answer with a nod and turns away from him without another word. On her back a sword is slung, and she seems to slump under the weight of it. Flax listens to the crunch of her boots on the charcoal grass as she draws away from him.

A knight. That will be a problem.

Flax scrapes the bark from a willow tree he finds, nursing it back to health just enough to help him. It is a single sprout of brown and grey against the blackened landscape.

He rushes back to the bird.

It is too late. The knight is aiming the crossbow, bolt already in place. The chaoswing screeches and flings its wings out.

Flax drops the willow bark onto the ashen ground and rushes between them, his hands thrusted up to the side to block the aim of the knight.

"It is sick!" he insists.

"Good," she snarls, with the false aggression of a kitten. "That means it will be easier to kill. I'd rather get rid of it before it gets stronger and burns the rest of the province."

"No," he tells her, hands still raised. "It is sick. It has a fever. It will... well, I do not know, but I believe it will be better once I help it." He feels fear and the heat of the chaoswing mix to slick him with sweat. It drips down the sides of his face, drops onto the ground below. Tiny sprouts form at his feet. He hopes the knight will not notice. He feels terrified of the cold metal she wields, how flippantly she brandishes her crossbow, even as her body trembles. She fears the monster she sees before her. He fears what she will do while afraid.

The knight glares at him for a moment – he cannot see her eyes, but he can feel the heat of her stare. Flax feels laid bare. He is not familiar with being so uncovered around humans. Usually, he at least wears a hat.

"What are you, anyways?" the knight asks as she lowers her crossbow. Her shoulders seem to slump slightly.

Flax lets out a sigh of relief. He can see the smoke disturbed around him, curling. "Some people say I am a witch," he explains dryly.

"Don't look like any witch I've seen before."

"And how many have you seen?"

The knight ignores him, leaning to look past his shoulder at the chaoswing. "I've never seen one of those before." He can hear the warble in her voice, the uncertainty.

"Neither have I," he admits. "It is a chaoswing."

"And how'd you know that?"

Flax does not want to try to explain the little voice in his head that is a remnant of the life he lived before, when he was not a dryad. He shrugs instead.

"You have three days to sort out this whole sick bird business before I come back and put a crossbow bolt through each of you," she tells Flax, voice filled with false bravado, and her helmet bobs as she nods at each of them. "And If I see it come south, I'll kill it immediately." He sees the way her back straightens with this resolution. He wants to say that he understands – that he will not tell anyone she came this way, that he understands her reticence towards harming a creature that does not seem to be actively trying to harm anyone. Three days is an acceptable length of time for a hard to track creature, and when the whole forest is in flames, a bird made of fire would normally be difficult to find, if it had kept flying. Three days and she can prepare for a fight to the death, shake off the fear that clouds her.

Flax glances back at the chaoswing. It does not seem ready to fly, so he figures he can relay the words of the knight after if the bird did not understand. He wonders if the knight has noticed the tiny, dancing flames on the chaoswing. Perhaps she only thinks they are feathers too.

The knight backs up, clearly not comfortable to turn away just yet.

"Wait," he tells her as he raises a hand. "The chaoswing is not from here. I need to know which way it can go. Which way the bird came from."

The knight looks up at the sky for a moment as she considers, consulting the directions written in the sky with the sun – barely visible through the smoke – before she turns her gaze back towards Flax. She raises her left hand with a slash. "Northeast," she says, and an unsteady finger points out the direction. "They said it came screaming out of the crystal mountains. Not like you can see them here, but it's that direction."

As soon as the knight leaves the clearing, Flax begins to brew.

The chaoswing recoils from water, so Flax has to condense down his tincture until it is a tar. Then he serves it up on a charcoal platter, winces at the heat, retreats. When the chaoswing coughs, spouts of flame leap from it. Flax feels a singe of flame across his back as he turns away. He retreats to the sooty stream and soaks himself.

Flax walks farther, northeast, as he tries to find the path. As he walks, he sweats and weeps, and flicks droplets across the ground. The soil bursts with life, ravenous, feeding on the new nutrients that are being fed to it. He finds that the river came from the north, and once he is far enough away the smoke is thin enough that he basks in the sun. He feels rejuvenated. It feels harder to return.

He knows he is pushing himself too far. He also knows that he will not stop until the bird is safe, or dead. Dead is easier, but the thought abhors him. And what will happen when the chaoswing dies? Might it explode?

And what of the little flamelings? Will they be consumed too? Or will they fly off in so many different directions, carrying their fires across the continent?

The third day came too quickly.

Flax begs the bird to fly. He is able to approach it easier now – it is no longer sweltering to be near. He is not sure if this is because his medicine is working, or if he is somehow used to the heat.

The little flamelings spin and twirl on the back of the chaoswing. They have many different shapes, flickering forms, as if they have not decided what creatures they want to be. They truly look like little flames, with tiny coal-black skeletal bodies. Flax notices the smallest one, the runt, hardly moves. He grows some grass and feeds it to the flamelings. They devour his offering hungrily.

The chaoswing is listless, hardly moving.

"You have to leave," he tells the chaoswing. "I found the way back, and I have grown a guiding trail for you to follow as far as I am able. Continue in that direction. The knight will return, and when it does, it will kill us all if you have not left."

"The knight has already returned," a grave, feminine voice says behind Flax. He hears the drawing of a string.

Flax is weak and he has no tears nor sweat left in him to give. But he knows he has one more way he can grow.

He takes a sharp piece of charcoal and slices across his palm. Blood, amber-coloured, pours from the wound and coats the forest floor, soaking into the earth. It forms a semi-circle facing away from him, towards the knight.

The knight stares at him. Flax let the blood drip and then clenches his hand into a fist.

Instantly trees sprout between him and the knight – massive trees with thick trunks, as close together as a fence. The knight screams – not in pain, but surprise.

"Please!" Flax shouts at the chaoswing. "Go!"

The bird looks at him with its coal-black eyes, then stretches out its wings until they are so close they almost touch him. From the other side of the trees, Flax can hear the knight hacking away – trying to get through the tangles of roots, the ensnaring branches.

The chaoswing beats its wings, and with a rush of air, launches into the sky.

Flax turns to watch its ascent, marveling at how the smoke seems to clear at its departure. He basks as the sun shines on his face – but then, as the chaoswing launches north-east, Flax sees something fall.

He rushes forward, diving to his knees to catch the falling ember before it hits the ground. He cradles it in his hands.

It is a flameling, the runt, the smallest. He sees that it is too young to fly on its own. It has not even developed wings; it is just a tiny wisp of flame.

Flax calls out, but the chaoswing does not hear. Or perhaps it does and ignores him – it has other children to carry, and the struggle of the knight behind him sounds like she is growing successful at freeing herself from the thicket. Flax stares at the tiny wisp in his hand.

This creature is antithetical to the dryad – flame and frond could never be brothers. A dryad cannot make a flame, no matter how hard they try – and Flax has tried many, many times. Flame burns, dryads grow, opposite forces, dichotomous in nature. And yet this smallest of the flamelings calls to him. He is not sure if it is some sort of previously latent paternal urge, like when he used to care for the other budding dryads and they would feed on his tears, but he knows in his heart he cannot leave it behind.

Flax imagines collapsing into a nearby river and floating down it to escape the knight, but the flameling would die. Instead, he runs in the direction opposite of which the chaoswing flies, blood droplets dripping, growing trees in his wake. He is faster than humans, and the knight is soon lost far behind. Flax does not think she will follow him, but if she does, he knows he will escape again. The blood that still drips from his body will protect him.

As he runs, he sees that just because the chaoswing is gone, it does not mean the forest fire has stopped. It has receded but not died, and continues to burn in the places where there is still trees for it to feast on. Massive swathes of land are nothing but blackened spikes, now crumbling into cinders. The destruction halts him.

Let it burn, the old part of him says. But Flax does not listen. He is a dryad in this life, despite his expulsion from the Unending Forest. Dryads grow plants. The soil thrives on their blood, sweat, and tears. Dryads are life, not just preserving, but flourishing. Not the rebirth the old him begs of the cinders that will litter this place, but regrowth. He will start this forest anew.

Flax does not mind his exhaustion as he follows the flames, growing new plants in their wake. He does not mind the smoke that weakens him, the sun that always seems to hide. He does not mind being so close to the flames.

Flax may be a dryad, but he now possesses flame.

One Breath of Hot, Toxic Gases Can Fatally Burn a Firefighter's Lungs and Airway.

by Tyree Corfe

slate covers my hands
my eyes
          to wash is
to scrub too deep
          to wash is
to feel sets of eyes on my back

          hoses of the day
          gush into the ground
          search & destroy

          all sense of embered life
do you smell it?
that moment

          Wandering patrols find
               the farm, abandoned
                    animal agriculture:
                    in the middle of the pen,
                         huddled char.

it still
          powders me
it still
          wont wash off

CHANGE TAKES TIME

By Kilmeny MacMichael

C asey was absolutely not thinking about Staats when she got his text.

they die it u fault

She looked up to see the reflection of the hair dresser doing a re-enaction of The Scream.

"Show me," Casey demanded, dealing with the immediate first.

The hair dresser reluctantly reached for a mirror. "It'll grow back..."

Casey's phone vibrated again.

How bad could it be?

She'd get plenty of feedback. It was amazing how many people called it open season on your appearance when you got in front of a camera.

"Sometimes, you just have to say you're sorry," The hair dresser said, positioning the mirror so Casey could see the damage. "Sorry."

Casey's brown eyes blinked at herself in the mirror, from her tanned, thin-browed, heart-shaped face. The undercut she'd requested was significantly more extensive than she'd wanted.

She started chewing her lower lip. Served her right for just walking into the first hair salon she saw. She should have checked the reviews.

She reread the text:

they die it u fault

Staats Joeseph. Rancher. Volunteer firefighter, sometimes tour guide. Five stars out of five, pending further investigation.

> *that's a terrible thing to say*

Staats was blond, although she was unsure if it was natural colour or not; with brown skin which would darken further as the summer went on. His eyes were Celtic hazel-green; quite fascinating when he came close enough to kiss. And his body... but, no, this was not the time.

> *what are you talking about*

> *hello*

> *u told them they could stay*

The people under evacuation orders? In the little subdivision outside of town?

> *they had the right*

> *now they're in trouble*

> *they have a right to get in trouble*

Legally, actually, no. Not after the local state of emergency was declared.

But morally? She stuck by it. Adults were adults and you should treat them as such.

She quit her job five days ago. People in trouble? Smelled like a story. Now that she was freelancing, she needed to chase things like this.

what you mean

gtg gt them

She thought she might spend a night of regret, following her resignation, but she found a Californian instead. It wasn't difficult. When she'd noted it was possible to place a different interpretation, instead of neighbourly friendliness, on the stars-and-stripes-flying fire vehicles parading across the border, she was called paranoid. Was she? These weren't city-fied coasties, these were the kind of men who talked about the state of Jefferson. She didn't mind them in bed, but she didn't want them to stay.

The people in the subdivision had stayed up there two outlaw nights already. What had changed this afternoon?

why

fire

Sherlock, of course there was a fire, what else would bring her here? It flared up a week ago. A slow response from authorities, citing strained resources due to other wildfires, closer to larger towns. You lived in a small town, you had to get used to being triaged at the bottom of the list. That was just the way it was.

Casey was on her feet, grabbing her purse from the counter, ignoring the hair dresser's further apologies.

?

Casey looked out onto the smoke-drenched main street of the town. Staats' small town.

> *fire was laying down this morning*

Staats replied:

> *r u stupid*

She didn't think she was. Part of the reason why she resigned. She was tired of sounding stupid, repeating the same lack-of-information over and over, serving up nothing but government lines. Don't upset anyone, don't get worried about anything. Above all, don't get angry.

She didn't know why they hadn't replaced all information officers with AI. All they seemed to want from them was repetition.

But she was human and she was angry.

> *i don't know what you're talking about*

There must be something going on. Staats was usually a polite dude. Unlike Casey, walking out of the hair dresser's without making a move to pay. No way was she paying for this.

Out on the street, she looked up towards the fire. She knew where it was, on a ridge above town, but the smoke was so heavy you couldn't even see the ridge. A little over half an hour ago, when she'd entered the salon, the air in town had been almost clear.

> *wind change*

That was the thing about fires, they could change their "minds." Did Staats remember the game they used to play?

> *scorpions*

For almost a month, two years ago, during the Conkle Lake fire, they'd kept up an exchange, in between working moments, sometimes with others joining in. Titles of songs, related to fire, or fire weather, the older the song the better. No repeats within a day. Loser drove an hour and a half into the nearest town to get pizza at the end of the week.

Casey usually won.

There were three people up at the subdivision, near the ridge, defying the evacuation orders. Yesterday Casey told the world about them, how they would and could stay and defend their homes. It was their decision and they said they understood the risks. If they wanted to risk being immolated...

Staats would go up and try and get them again. He was one of those infuriating people who believed you shouldn't ask anyone to do anything you wouldn't do yourself.

leave them

called for help

Well, now they weren't resilient do-it-yourself heroes, now they were grade A buttholes. And Staats was going to help them. And maybe it was...

It wasn't her fault. But...

you're too nice

She got into her van, noting she needed to get a new "Beware: Live Snakes" sticker for her door, and turned on her dashcam, then her voice to text.

take me with you

no

She started her van up.

where are you

She started driving towards the highway. Turn left, turn right...

here

The oversized black pick-up with the volunteer fire department badge rumbled by.

i'm coming with you

i caused the problem let me fix it

She was on Staats' bumper like gum on the hem of a new pair of pants.

Traffic was light and she glanced around for her face mask.

The fire they were approaching was first spotted not far off the highway several kilometers from town. There were no lightning strikes reported in the previous forty-eight hours. "Under investigation," Casey had been required to read out. For previous such fires, she'd managed to supress her eye-rolls, but for this one, she let her eyeballs shake and rattle all over the live stream.

They pulled into a lane marked off by traffic cones, followed it around a corner with a barricade half across the intersection.

She'd done her job, she'd communicated, she repeated the obvious advice. Against throwing cigarettes out of your car windows, driving over dried-up landscapes, having campfires. Advice on how not to be a bonehead.

Her former boss had reprimanded her. Apparently "bonehead" was not approved vocabulary.

She hadn't mentioned fire fighters as arsonists, or weather balloons as updated Fu-Gos, the top two conspiracy theories in town. Her boss didn't show any gratitude for such restraint.

Staats was pulling ahead. Casey's van was designed for living in, not for racing. Ash had started to fall across her windshield.

the racoons

Perhaps Staats knew the people in the subdivision personally.

Casey lived out of her van. But Staats had a home. It wasn't in immediate danger but it wasn't out of danger from this fire, either. Someone – some idiot – who would probably never be found – and would never be held responsible – might take Staat's home away.

The day after her livestream eye-rolling incident, Casey had gone further off script, "A thousand hectares. You might be thinking, great, so, Casey, what actually is a hectare? I can give you the math definition, but let me do something you can actually imagine. Here it is in Canadian Tires."

It was felt by Casey's boss this was unapproved promotion of a private company. But her view count increased. She continued to gain positive comments.

They had started up hill, leaving town.

Her message, inspired by an early morning encounter, on the day before she resigned?

"Look, buddy, if you're riding your dirt bike out into the trees right now? You're either a complete idiot or malicious. Either way you should be stopped."

This, she was told, was both unprofessional and a potential incitement to violence. She invited her ex-boss to jump in the nearest, coldest, lake.

And now, she had her own content channel, with advertising dollars already coming in. She could say what she wanted to say.

Braking, they had come to the end of the open road. Two Mountie cars created a roadblock ahead, preventing further passage.

Staats parked. Casey clunked her van into neutral. Staats got out and walked over to the officers, talked. Should she get out? Should she put her mask on if she did get out? People responded better to faces.

But being downwind of this fire, they were likely experiencing some of the worst air quality in the world. When a wild fire burns at its fiercest it boils creeks and fish and laughs out benzene and formaldehyde. N95 masks or respirators help for as long as their filters don't clog, for as long as you can keep them tight against your face as you sweat and move. But they do not solve the actual problem. And your eyes still get stung.

A maskless Staats and the masked Mounties came to some kind of agreement.

Staats walked over to the van, scowling, and made an angry gesture. She lowered her window.

"Take me with you," she said.

The Mounties were getting into one car and moving it up the road.

"If I asked you to stay here, would you?"

"No."

"You could get hurt."

"So could you."

Staats wasted a few more moments glaring at her. "All right. We'll take my truck."

"Yessir," she said, grabbing her camera off the passenger seat. His eyebrows shot up but he got into his driver's seat without further comment.

"Still using diesel, huh?"

Staats did not reply. They followed the pair of Mounties past a second, sawhorse barricade. The road passed several small, animal-less hobby farms.

The road curved into a steep climb away from the valley floor, trees crowding in. Casey glanced up the hill and saw fire.

"Uhh..."

"I see it," Staats said, and pressed a little harder on the accelerator. The Mountie flashed their lights and stepped on it themselves.

They came to a plastic picket fence and a sign announcing the Sunshine West Ridge Estates.

To the right of the sign, standing as still as a statue, was an ostrich.

"Ostrich," Casey said as they passed through the gate in the fence.

"What?"

"There was an ostrich."

Staats slowed down, looking in the rear-view mirror. Casey turned in her seat. No ostrich.

"Very funny," Staats said.

"I pinkie swear. There was."

They drove on.

The "estate" was unlikely to ever bustle, mostly housing retirees in newer yet modest bungalows, duplexes and rowhouses. But under ordinary circumstances, during the day, you would expect to see a couple of people about, maybe walking a dog, or getting ready to golf.

Today there was no-one on the streets.

Someone had left a swimsuit and towel out on a clothes line, and someone else had their flag up on a pole in their front yard, snapping away. There were a lot of cedar bushes planted between the houses, marking the property lines.

"I don't know why people keep planting cedars," Casey said to say something. There were less thirsty, less flammable choices, less likely to be "pruned" by deer.

Staats replied. "It's hard to teach old dogs new tricks."

She glanced at him. Who was the dog in this relationship?

They turned a corner and at the end of the street where the woods started, they could see flames.

"Dang."

Staats came to a hard stop behind the cop car, then did a three-point turn, putting the fire behind them. He kept the truck running. No idle free BC.

There was a small sprinkler rotating on the roof of a bungalow with a tall wooden fence. This is where the Williams lived.

"Stay in the truck," Staats said.

Casey nodded and waited for him to go up the driveway and knock on the front door before hopping out, camera in hand. She immediately missed the truck's air conditioning.

Mr Ethelbert lived in one half of a false adobe duplex at the end of this street. The old man in plaid shirt sleeves and a wide brimmed hat was looking over his backyard, turning and smiling when he recognized her.

"Hello Miss Vanvuur," he said. "What happened to your hair?"

"Never mind," she said, and then sneezed. She looked over his backyard towards the fire.

"Er, Mister Ethelbert…"

Mr Ethelbert said, "I'm ready to go."

She looked at him.

"It's not just women who can change their minds," he said. "What's with your hair?"

"Never mind," she said again.

"I've decided to take only myself and this here," he said, gesturing to a small strongbox. "I'm going to leave my car. I've been wanting a new car. I figure I can hitch a ride with you."

"Sure," she said. She wasn't an insurance investigator.

The fire seemed to be having trouble coming over a little ditch. Casey figured there was some flame retardant laid down there. She also figured it wouldn't last.

Mr Ethelbert carried his box over to Staats' truck, cheerfully gave the Mounties the finger, and hopped into the truck bed.

The Mounties had clearly decided they were not leaving their vehicle unless absolutely necessary. Breathing the smoke was starting to make her stomach hurt, so Casey couldn't blame them.

Meanwhile, Staats was with the Williams on their front steps. Casey walked over with her camera on.

"I don't want to leave without Zak," Lisa Williams was saying as Larry Williams trundled two rolling suitcases out their door. A cry came from a pet carrier at the top of the steps.

"Who is Zak?" Staats asked.

"Is he an ostrich?" Casey asked. "Because I saw an ostrich."

"That must have been Irma," Lisa said. "Zak is a cat."

"We got Paulie at least," Larry said.

"Okay, we're taking one cat, and missing one cat?" Staats asked.

"We almost had Zak an hour or so ago, but then he ran out the back."

"Who does Irma the ostrich belong to?" Casey asked, checking she had the group nicely framed in the picture. She could grab stills later, when she got back to her van and laptop.

"I think she's a rhea."

"A what?"

"Looks like a small ostrich."

"We don't have time for an ostrich," Staats said.

"I thought you liked birds," Casey said.

"What are we going to do about Zak?" Lisa said.

The Mounties honked their horn.

Staats said, "Leave some food and water out for him. As soon as possible, I'll get someone in to look for him. But we need to leave."

"He must be so scared," Lisa said.

"I'm sorry," Staats said.

"You've got one, right? And it's not like there's a shortage of cats," Casey said.

"Excuse me?"

"You can always get another. The shelters are full of them."

"She doesn't have pets," Staats offered.

This was true. The snake habitat in her van was for show. She liked the look on people's faces when they came in and noticed the fully equipped snake habitat was empty, the lid partially opened. It was, of course, a test.

Some people came up with excuses to leave. Some people became extra excited. Some people didn't seem to notice at all.

Staats had simply asked about it, and she had told him the truth.

Anyway, pets were a liability during fire season. She learned that when she was fourteen.

Staats was saying, "I understand. I have pigeons. I promise you; we'll look for Zak. He's probably a smart cat. Smart enough to escape, right? If we see him, we'll take care of him."

"You have pigeons?"

"Yes."

"He races them," Casey added. "Has a whole house built for them on his ranch."

"That's right. I like animals. More than some people. I give you my personal word, I will come back and try and find Zak."

"There really isn't any more that we can do," Larry Wilson said.

"All right," Lisa said.

"Thank you."

Staat's phone started ringing. He turned it off. Casey recorded them getting into the truck, panning the camera back over the house and street, slowing down to bring the flames again into focus. Unless she was very much mistaken, Mr Ethelbert's back lawn was now on fire. The Mounties drove past.

Staats revved his engine. Casey hurried around to the passenger door. There was no way she was going to fit in there with them, with Lisa Wilson carrying the cat carrier on her lap.

Casey had never ridden in the back of a truck before. If she could lean on the cab to steady her arms and hands, she would be able to use the camera...

"Sit down, young lady," Mr Ethelbert said from where he was sitting in the truck bed.

She sat. It was not all that comfortable.

It became less comfortable as Staats chased the Mountie car back down the road.

The ride out to Staats' home two years ago had been beautiful, the valley uncommonly green. The sky was clear, and the roast chicken dinner from the deli counter sent warmth through the vehicle.

They had dinner in his kitchen as a sun shower sparkled the air. When it stopped, he showed her around the small ranch he shared with his absent brothers. They added freshly shucked corn cobbs to the meal. The long evening opened itself as she got to see Staats smile, releasing a basket of young racing pigeons from his far fence line. The iridescent birds wheeled and turned and streaked back to their roost. She thought she would make him smile even more, later, that night.

She was too sure of herself. Too aggressive. Too greedy.

He called her a rank six fire. All consuming and far too dangerous to touch.

Unfair. A rank five, maybe. Indirect attack and planned ignitions to remove fuel in the path. Keep escape routes in mind.

With Staats, she didn't want to burn that fast. It was fun but maybe it was why everyone was living like this now, running from fire to fire, while lost and frightened ostriches roamed the land. She didn't want to break Staats.

Staats was an overwintering fire. Not much to see, but keeping alive even under feet of freezing snow. Unexpectedly tenacious, unexpectedly vulnerable.

When she went to look for drinking glasses in his cupboards, she found his medication.

"Not a secret," he said, "But I'd appreciate you didn't spread it around."

She hadn't. She wasn't a monster.

She couldn't see where they were going, sitting backwards in the truck. Mr Ethelbert had one liver-spotted hand on top of his strongbox and the other holding his hat.

Casey cradled her camera between her knees.

All she could see was the neighbourhood scrolling away from them. Paradise Street. The street with the swimsuit. The main boulevard into the complex. All disappearing into smoke.

Irma the bird.

Grey-brown, a bit fluffy looking, feathers being tossed about in the wind.

"Hey!" Casey shouted. "Hey, stop the truck!"

Staats did not stop the truck. They passed the fence.

Saving Irma wasn't going to save her anyway. Not with Staats. Even if he did like birds.

"What happened to your hair?" Mr Ethelbert asked again.

"A mistake."

He nodded. "Maybe you should dye it."

She wasn't sure how that would help.

"Lots of folks like colour these days. I'll bet if you put enough funky colour in it, people will think the accident was on purpose."

"You could be right."

The truck slowed. The truck crawled along.

Casey didn't want to die.

She put her camera down, hoping it wouldn't rattle too far.

Staats brought the truck to a halt. Casey tried to peer through the slider window, past the people and cat in the cab, and out the front. It could have been easier. She stood up.

An aspen colony on the left-hand side of the road was on fire – flames licking up the papery trunks, shaking leaves burning off. The Mountie car was edging through, swerving around blowing, flaming leaves and cinders.

Casey reached for her camera, thought better of it. She knocked on the window.

Staats slid it open. "I'm afraid we've reached Plan D, Case."

Casey noted there was sweat making its way down the side of Staat's face, near his ear. Plan B was always think of Plan C. And Plan D was run like all heck.

"There's no other way out?"

"No."

"That's ridiculous." Her voice pitched up.

"I didn't build it."

"Can this thing go off road?"

"Not down a mountain, it can't."

"Well, what if we just got out? Walked around?"

"Casey, do you really think we can outrun this fire if it..."

The Mountie ahead jammed brakes as an aspen collapsed in front of their car.

"Oh my God."

No one spoke as they watched the police back up, then crawl around the burning tree. There was barely enough space on the right-hand shoulder to get by.

Casey swallowed hard around a dry clog in her throat. "Staats, just drive. Just follow them and drive."

"But it's not safe."

"And the alternative is...?"

Mr Ethelbert said, "We can go back to my place. I don't mind."

Staats drummed his fingers against the steering wheel. "Maybe they can get a helicopter to us..."

"From where? Just go. Plan D like you said."

"Sheltering in place may be the best..."

A shower of embers fell across the truck.

Casey thumped the window. "Drive, or let me do it!"

More finger drumming from Staats. The Mountie car disappeared around a corner.

To hell with this, Casey thought. I'm not going to go back and die in an old man's false-fronted bungalow. She grabbed her camera, checked the focus, and handed it to Mr Ethelbert.

"Point it at things that seem exciting," she said. He pointed it back at her. He was a nice old man. She hopped over the side of the truck.

The drop was longer than expected, her feet protested, but she didn't let them distract.

She tugged on the driver's side door. Nothing happened. "I'm serious," she said to Staats, "Drive this thing or…" she trailed off, listening.

Above the sounds of the fire there was honking.

She could feel her heart. "Staats, they made it. The Mounties made it. We can make it too. This is not the time for you to freeze. Are you frozen?"

"I'm going back."

"No, listen!"

The cat complained in its carrier. The honking continued.

"Hear that? They don't sound very far. They're telling us to come through!"

"You don't know that."

They sat there, idling, as poplars popped open. It was hot. Casey mashed her teeth against her lip, trying to think of how to get Staats to go.

"You know someone else will try and come get us if we don't get ourselves out. Do you want to make it worse?"

He wiped his face with his shirt. "This is why when we say evacuate, we mean evacuate. Why it's not a suggestion."

"Fine, can we have our learning moment later, please?"

Lisa Wilson was starting to cry. Staats sighed. "All right. But it's my truck. I'll drive."

Casey couldn't haul herself back into the truck bed from the side, so she had to go and find a wheel to stand on first.

"Casey?" Staats called.

"Yeah?"

"I… I like your hair."

She banged her knee getting back in.

In the introduction to her carefully edited, audio-free, channel exclusive video, Casey gave full credit to Mr Ethelbert. He kept the camera more or less steady.

She edited herself out, sitting back down in the corner closest to Staats, drawing her knees up and tucking her head down into her arms, closing her eyes.

Only through the camera, later, did she see the truck back up ten feet, pull as far right as it could, to the edge of the road, the drop below no more than two feet off.

And then the acceleration, the yards of flaming debris flurrying past.

She also cut the video when they reached the road block, when she got out of the truck, walked over to her waiting van and threw up.

But she did include a later and rehearsed moment, when she walked up to the police officers, and Staats, and told them she was sorry.

She told Staats she was sorry.

A helicopter beat up and over and past them, lugging a bucket. It sounded tired.

That night at the RV park, while she waited for the yellow and red dye to set into her hair, she got her answer, from Staats.

run with us – lisa lougheed

And Casey ordered the pizza.

SMOKE AND TEARS

By Lesley Hebert

82   RED EYES AND TIRED LUNGS

The low grey sky
hides the mountainous horizon.
My nose wrinkles against the acrid smoke
that stings my weeping eyes.

Do you weep for humanity
if smoke gets in your eyes?

The world is burning.
The firestorm is here.
My lungs, finally clean of nicotine,
now choke on ash and creosote.

Will you weep for humanity
when smoke gets in your eyes?

I remember the sulphur stench of 1952.
Only four,
I wrapped a scarf around my face,
held my mother's hand
and walked blind
through London's great green killer smog.
I know this hellish air may well get worse.
Choking nausea hits my gut.

I weep for humanity
as smoke gets in my eyes.

SMOKE HURTS

BY HILMA SINKINSON

Another flying colour! Must chase it! Hazel calls them butterflies, but that is a big word. I have never caught this little bird-like thing. It is great fun though as I dodge and weave trying to catch one. It is bright orange and big for a butterfly. I guess I will have to give up. It heads off into the distance. Bounding back to the house, I get a big drink from the water dish Hazel put out for me this morning. It has a little tap in the middle and water bubbles up all the time. It is better than the dish I had before that dried up really fast. Heading down to the grass, I stretch out in the sun for a snooze. Frank is in the building where the tools are, and Hazel is in the house. All is quiet and peaceful.

It's nice remembering days like this. Lately, there have been very few butterflies or birds. The sky is filled with heavy white smoke. I thought it was a fluffy cloud until I heard Frank and Hazel call it smoke. It smells terrible. Each day it has been getting thicker and thicker. My humans say it is a forest fire. They sound worried that it is coming closer. For the last few days they were hauling boxes out to the travel trailer we take camping. I don't like the smoke. It keeps stinging my throat and my eyes.

Frank is having problems with the smoke, more than Hazel and I. We would play with the ball in the yard every night. He never got tired, but I sure did. Then I would lay down by his chair on the porch and he would read. He used to use his white tank and tubes only at night. Now, he never stays outside for very long. He is using the tubes first thing in the morning and frequently during the day. He seems to be out of breath and moving very slow. I have been allowed to sleep in the house on my bed every night. That usually happens when it snows, not when it is hot outside.

Frank and Hazel came onto the deck and stood looking up at the hills behind the house. They were talking loud and quick. When I looked up I saw dark smoke rising from the hills. That was strange. As we watched I saw bits of orange and red flickering. I heard my humans talking, and I could feel their worry. Instead of coming into the yard to play ball with me, Frank sat down shaking his head. That was a signal to me that I was doing something wrong. I felt so confused.

I moved up to Frank, putting my head on his knee. Looking down at me, he shook his head, and there were tears in his eyes. "We'll be ok, Rex. It's a forest fire coming towards us. We may have to leave. You're a good dog."

Hazel had rushed into the house to answer the bells that were ringing. She called to Frank about "get ready". That got Frank moving into the house. As I sat watching, I couldn't help but feel a little scared. Hazel had gotten a box and was putting things from the kitchen into it including food from the fridge. Those all were taken into the trailer. A nasty burning smell was in my nose and throat. It seemed to be coming from the cloud that was moving across the field towards the house. As it got closer, my eyes were burning, and my throat was scratchy.

Every few minutes either Frank or Hazel would come to the deck. They would look up at the hills, which got harder and harder to see in the cloud. Shaking their heads they would go back inside and rush around some more. Frank started putting things in the truck. He then backed up to the trailer we used on trips away from home. He towed the trailer up to the front of the house. He kept moving boxes into the truck and the trailer, sitting down after each trip with the tubes. I laid down on the porch and watched.

It was supper time when Frank called me into the house. Even though I drank a lot of water, my throat did not feel better. My food scratched my throat and breathing was a struggle. That night we didn't play with my ball. We didn't sit outside on the deck. The cloud was so thick and smelled so bad that my throat ached. Frank and I were both coughing.

Morning came suddenly as Frank answered the bells by his bed. I heard him say, "Ok. We're ready. We'll be leaving within the hour." Before he even hung up, Hazel was diving out of bed. Both of them rushed into their clothes and gathered up bags. Calling me, Frank said, "Come on Rex. No time for breakfast right now. We are leaving." As he headed downstairs, I followed. I was definitely confused. My throat wasn't as bad this morning, but it was still scratchy. I coughed a lot when I went outside to pee.

In no time at all, I was in the truck with the two backpacks. There were more boxes and things loaded into the trailer. I saw my food dish and water dish loaded up with a bag of my food. Instead of happy smiles, both Frank and Hazel looked very worried. They kept looking out at the smoke. It was really thick. I could see more orange streaks in the cloud down at the ground. None of us could breath without coughing. Frank had put the cold fan on in the truck, and the doors were closed.

As we were driving down the road away from the cloud, Frank started to cough. He pulled over to the side of the road. Hazel took his place driving while he sat sipping water between coughs. He then put the tubes in his nose, still fighting to stop coughing. When we got to the big road, there were lots of trucks, including some with bright lights flashing. There was a guy in bright yellow wearing a scary mask waving one vehicle at a time onto the main road. I had never seen so many cars, trucks, and trailers. We were all going in one direction. Frank couldn't talk at all, so Hazel was the only voice in the truck. She kept saying, "Get going, people!" "Move!" "Hurry up!" She sounded scared.

Even with the windows closed, I could smell the smoke. My eyes were watering and my throat felt raw. Frank was struggling to breath in the tubes. Hazel was looking worried, and constantly checking on Frank. I closed my eyes and slept. When I woke up Hazel was parking us on the side of a parking lot. There was a big tree providing me with shade. She tied me to the tree and put my filled water dish out. She had to shake Frank to wake him up. He didn't look good. Hazel left the truck and rushed into a big building, coming out with a chair on wheels. Frank was soon in the chair. Shutting the door, Hazel called, "Good boy, Rex. Lay down. We'll be back."

I watched the building for awhile, but when they didn't come back out, I curled up to sleep. It was getting hot. It was still smoky here, but I could see further. I checked my water dish, but it was empty. My eyes were still burning, and my throat was terrible. I went back to sleep.

Finally! Frank and Hazel were back. Frank was in the chair still, but he looked better now. Hazel got him settled and drove us out of the parking lot. I heard them talking that we would be at the campground in an hour. I was looking forward to getting out. I needed more water, and I really needed to lift my leg!

It seemed forever, but we got to a campground. Hazel went in a building to get a paper. We went to a shady site down the road. The air was clear here, so I could breathe again. As soon as we were parked, Hazel took me out of the truck. She tied me to a tree at the back of the lot where there were lots of trees and bushes. I dove for the closest tree and felt relief. Hazel brought my water dish over, filled to the top, and my food dish. Frank was moving slowly around the site, sitting down frequently. He was using the tubes, and the tank was on his back.

That night I got to sleep outside again. Although the air was much better, I started coughing. No matter how hard I tried to stretch my head out, I couldn't stop. I was finding it hard to breath, and my legs shook when I stood up. My eyes were watering and I could hardly see out of them. Hazel tried to get me to drink water, but I couldn't. As I dropped into my bed Hazel sat down beside me. She placed a fan on the ground that blew air across my hair. It actually felt good. Finally my coughing eased enough that I could sleep.

The next few days were terrible for me. My eyes were burning, making it hard to see. I felt so weak. I could hardly stand to drink my water. Food did not even tempt me. I used to dive into my food dish and finish it right away. Now, a couple of bites hurt so much, I just stopped eating. I slept all the time. When I tried to stand, my legs would shake, and the coughing would come back. At least the air felt clear.

Frank and Hazel were both worried about me. They were surprised at how much the smoke had affected me. I heard them call a dog doctor, called a vet. Hazel said they could take me to the vet's office to get oxygen if I found it too difficult to breath. She said something about a needle and IV fluids. I know a vet likes to stick me with needles every time I see them. I didn't want to go there.

Frank came out and set his chair in the shade by me. Petting my head he said, "Well boy, I could share my oxygen with you. I know you would feel better. My doctor would have a fit, and Hazel would get mad at me. I had no idea you could get so sick. I thought you would be low on the ground. The smoke shouldn't have been that bad. We are all finding this hard. So far, our house is still ok. The fire hasn't crossed the field in front of our property. Other homes have burned though. It will be tough to go home to, but I really want to." Too weak to stand long, I laid down at his feet and fell asleep.

We stayed at the campground for days. Hazel said it was 3 weeks. I was super sick. But the last few days, I felt so much better. I still found it hard to breath, but better. I could even go for walks with Frank and Hazel. My eyes were back to normal, and I seemed to have gotten my appetite back.

Who knew that I would suffer from the smoke I breathed? Frank and Hazel talked about it with a woman who knows dogs. She told us that it could affect me up to a day or two after I breathed in the smoke. Usually there would be coughing (right, I know that), sore eyes that would look red, and weakness. I hate to admit it, but my bed is still really comfortable these days. I seem to sleep all day and all night. There is nothing but fresh water, food, cool air, and sleep. I was glad I didn't have to visit the vet for a needle.

During this time, Frank seemed to be sick just like me. He used the tubes every day for hours. His cough seemed better. Last night we even played with my ball. We sat outside and listened to a radio play music. Occasionally Hazel would look at her little tv that lit up at night. It replaced the bells, I think. It would sing a song, and Hazel would talk into it. She shared that the forest fire was moving in a different direction, and we would be able to go home tomorrow.

Arriving home was not what I expected. There was still smoke in the air, but not as much as when we left. Our house was just as we had left it, except for the ash. Everywhere there were layers of ash. It poofed up when I walked and made me sneeze. Even on the deck, under the roof, there was ash. Inside the house was better. After I had ran to the bushes, also covered in ash, Hazel put me in the house and gave me my water dish. She told me I had to stay inside for now. That was actually a relief. Just coming home had tired me out.

Hazel and Frank moved in and out of the house, resting between each trip. Frank was having trouble breathing again. He probably needed to sneeze, just like me. My eyes were watering and my breathing was instantly better inside. Hazel made tea, but instead of sitting out on the porch, they sat at the kitchen table. They were tired. I could tell. Neither one talked, just looked down at their tea cup.

I moved over and placed my head on Frank's knee. He reached down and pet me on the head. Over and over, his hand smoothed down my head, neck, and onto my back. He shook his hand and said to Helen; "He needs a bath".

"Yes. I guess we all need baths. The house also needs a good wash, inside and out. Do you think we could hire someone to give us a hand outside? You can't be out there stirring up the ashes. I can't do both, and the sooner done the better."

"I'll call around. We have some young men around that may be willing to help out for cash."

I moved back to my bed. Even it smelled of smoke, but it was comfortable. I fell into a deep sleep. I was tired out from the travel. I also hadn't fully recovered my energy since the smoke sickness.

I awoke later coughing and coughing. Hazel came over and brought me fresh water and waved a wet towel around the room. It did move the dust around, but I could feel cool air again. She reached down and took my bed from under me. Moving quickly she took it into the washing room and put it in the big washer. She was muttering about everything needing to be washed. She got the washer started and pulled things out of the dryer. I looked around for Frank. Hazel told me he was upstairs on the bed having a rest. My coughing was slowing down, but my chest was hurting, and my throat was burning.

Hazel called me upstairs and into their bathroom. I knew what was coming. I had gotten into some rotten smells before and had to take a bath. I didn't mind the water, but I felt exhausted by the time she was rinsing me off. She let me have a good shake after toweling me off. Then she called me into the bedroom. Frank had his mask on. The tank was hissing softly and Hazel checked it before adjusting the mask. He didn't even wake up. I crawled up on the bed very slowly. Hazel told me no very firmly, but when I laid my head across Frank's legs, she gave up. With tears in her eyes she turned and left the room.

It took a long time for both Frank and I to get active again. I couldn't run very far before stopping and coughing. With all the ash around, there was no where to go without smelling smoke. Frank seemed the same. He used the mask all the time outside, and the tubes inside. I got to stay in the house most of the time.

A young man came over and helped clean the outside of the house, the porch, and the yard. Hazel and Frank washed every wall and floor in the house. My bed smelled fresh and clean. We even got to sit out on the porch again. The air was getting cooler and the rain kept the smoke away. The fires had moved out of our area entirely. Soon I would be racing around, chasing the ball again. Frank had the twinkle back in his eyes and seldom used the mask now. Life was getting back to normal.

I knew all was good when I saw the birds and butterflies return to the yard. I still couldn't chase them, but I loved to watch them flitting about the garden. Yes, good days were here again.

Into the Great Unknown

by Asha Jade Goodwin

Born at the end of a cigarette
Curling, flaking, full of regret
Exhaling tar and tobacco
Dropping ash into the lap below
A sweet life, three inches long
Crooning my smoky song
Pinched between pursed lips two
Clasped between bent fingers who
Flicked me into the great unknown.

Buffeted by wind
Like a ballet dancer spinned
To the ditch where lay
A curve of earth for me to stay
What should have been my grave.

But still I burned, alive
With parched plants I did strive
Last year's leaves left to smother
Sun bit browned as another
Summer season starts to stink.

Born anew among dead flowers
Branches crumble under towers
Of thirsty trees, all the same
Planted side by side to tame
A forest, wild and free

What a great place for me to be
From a flicker to a flame
To a blaze, to a craze
Hunger sears me
Dry heat steers me
Into the underbrush below.

I grow hungry, breathing
Consuming, only feeding
My place in this world decided
By a chance encounter collided
With a stash of tinder left to dry
Underneath a heat dome sky
Quietly I crackle please
Give me more of these dry leaves!
Instead I feed upon the bark
I grow bright as it grows dark
Only a summer flame today
Spreading limbs begin to play
The world around grows ever hotter
Trees explode to be my fodder
I once sung tobacco and tar
Now in my wake I leave a scar
As I exhale there's no sky to see
But that would never bother me
I take this once quiet abode
My embers wild seeds sowed
To reach where I cannot go
The wind, my saviour, blow

My children into the great unknown.

I flush with indignation
Crackling on a water station
Brown and yellow bees swarming
Even as the air is warming
I hiss as I am kissed
Water to steam in this tryst
They draw a line, beat me back
Covered faces, they attack
With water and flame, no fellow friend
Try to starve me to my end
I turn away.

As I pull myself together
My path chosen by the weather
No feathers, ash is falling hard
Left behind my calling card
Pinched between roadways two
Clasped between two rivers who
Release me into the great unknown.

FLAMEBOUND

By Topper Sundquist

The fire spoke, and Elias Trilby listened.

Soot streaked Elias' scabbed elbows as he lay in front of the hearth, a chorus line of flames dancing in his eyes. His little dirt-blackened feet kicked dreamily, bony legs protruding from ill-fitting hand-me-down bib overalls. His brothers and sisters stepped over him as they trudged through their chores. By the time the sun disappeared from the lone easterly window overlooking the tomato patch and shone through the lone westerly window facing the endless spruce, his sides were bruised from the mostly-accidental kicks he received.

When Tansy's precious blanket, padded with real cotton and ordered special from the Montgomery Ward catalogue, burned to ashes, Elias gladly gave his over. Tansy pouted and screeched, for that was not HER blanket, HERS had the blue flowers and the real cotton, but she was promised a new one before the next year's snow blew. Elias produced some sacks he'd hidden away through the autumn and made himself a little nest in front of the hearth rather than share a bed with his brothers, promising never to let the coals surrender to Old Man Winter.

When a grassfire raced through the upper paddock in the spring, sending the cattle thundering through the buck-and-rail and taking Father and Mason away for days to retrieve them, Elias didn't bother trying to lie about his hand in it. From that day on he was always under the eye of one sibling or another, and the hide leashes were untrunked and put back into use around his ankles when days were busy.

When the rainbarrel caught fire in midsummer, Elias found himself over Father's knee, being calmly and deliberately switched up and down until sooty tears bled from his eyes. The days had been hazy and smothering, relentless baking heat curling the roof shingles and sending half-starved foxes raiding the coops with singular determination. Elias never admitted that he wanted to see if the rainwater ghosts would keep the barrel from burning, but it seemed that their protective powers were indeed limited.

They shouted at him, demanding explanations, but Elias could give none that they could understand. When little Alice passed early in the year from crisscross fever, the shouting lessened and their attention would wander. When they buried a brokeneck Tansy scarcely a week after the rainbarrel incident, Mother would often scream at him for no reason while Father would just... stare.

After that, he could endure the lethargic kicks as he lay in front of the fire, chin in his hands, feet swaying like reeds. He almost seemed to fade from family memory. At mealtimes, food was left out rather than served up for him. His clothes got scrubbed when he remembered to sneak them into Mother's reed basket on wash day. He still helped with meal times, but he moved as a spirit of the wind might, appearing here and there to offer a favor; rarely acknowledged, never thanked.

Summer stretched long in the daytime as the months passed, even as winter licked at their heels come nightfall. Most mornings found the fields dusted with frost, dew dripping and steaming from the eaves and tugging at the high, bone-dry branches of the black spruce, but by late afternoon the heat drove the family to hide under apple trees in the sparse little orchard or to make the trek down to the slow, muddy river.

No-one noticed when Elias started napping during the warmest times of the day, so he could stay awake, alert and alone during the empty doldrums of deepest night. The frost etched twisted figures on the windows with the sound of teeth rattling. When the northwind would slink out through the trees, squeezing their little log abode until the timbers creaked, sending its little shrieking messengers down the chimney, Elias would crawl as close to the fire as he could bear, which was very close indeed. His tanned cheeks were now ruddy from the near-constant burns, his unkempt hair shortened by simply singeing off the longest stragglers.

The words, Elias could hear the *words!* In his dreams he could remember the speech of the fire, remember and understand the strange language, but his waking mind betrayed him. The words were unintelligible in the waking world, so faint as to be doubtful he'd heard them at all, but he knew. He knew. He might not know the words, they might not even be words as he knew them, but he understood the sentiment, the feeling, the fear and the meaning.

He blinked furiously, so close he could feel his nostrils cracking, feel his protruding front teeth heating up and sending red hot pokers into the backs of his eyes. The coals from a dozen lays of birch and mountain pine formed a vast plain of velvety black, across which the still-burning splits of wood crackled and breathed. Elias studied the intricately carved, shifting hills and valleys of soot and embers, darkest sable dusted with silvery ash like shimmering curtains, crags and caves of orange and red and gold pounding in time with his heart. The mysterious but surely all-knowing songs of the fire echoed from these caves, coming not from a pinkie's width into the wood as his siblings claimed, but from miles and miles uncountable.

The buckles on his coveralls burned his chest, but he didn't notice. Elias licked his palm and scrubbed it across his ear, turning his head and craning closer still. It steamed away almost instantly, but in that moment he heard the Offer.

He glanced over his shoulder, immediately wincing as the cool air struck his heat-baked face. Snores and sighs and the crinkle and rustle of blankets wafted out from the looming black void that led to the bed room. Elias held his breath, squinting and trying to chase away the blue and green blobs of afterfire that dogged his vision.

When he stuck his hand into the fire there was pain, sudden and brilliant, and yet... not as bad as he'd feared. In fact, it was a struggle not to laugh. Fear! Why should he have been afraid? Fire feared nothing, not even the approach of what was surely to be a gloriously smothering winter, so why should he?

He allowed himself a giggle as his skin blistered and burned. A hundred tiny hairs flared to brief incandescence, turning to black ash to be devoured by the hungry, singing aurora of flame. He pushed deeper, one fingernail curling and twisting. He understood the Offer perfectly. Tears dug troughs through the soot on his cheeks, but his smile only deepened.

And then...

And then the Flame leapt, a birdlike flicker from an impossible distance to land on his fingertip. Elias nearly jerked his hand back, but the first faint twitch caused the Flame to tremble, on the verge of retreating. It took all his focus to withdraw his hand with the care and slowness of Mother stitching up Father's cheek after the incident with the whetstone.

The back of his hand wept pus, blisters outgrowing blisters. His fingers curled with aching, chary speed, the wrinkles at his knuckles cracking like parchment paper. The pain was an audible, furious thing, a continuous thunderclap beating at his skull, but it was a secret thing, something new and novel, something to be treasured. The prize, after all, peered out from between his middle two fingers.

He turned his hand over, cupping his fingers even as tiny droplets of blood spattered and sizzled on the hearth. There, precious and proud and more alive than Elias had ever imagined, more alive than his family sleeping not a dozen paces away, was the Flame.

"Hello," Elias whispered, a hoarse, parched wheeze.

The Flame whispered back, dancing in Elias's eyes.

***

Elias filched two eggs before dawn, cracking them behind the coop and using a mudbrush to gently daub the clear fluid on his poor burned hand. The secret pain he'd been granted, the privilege of allowing his hand to enter the fire, had been replaced by a gnawing, snaggletoothed thing, maddening and ceaseless. That was fine; he bore no ill will to the Flame, dancing curiously next to him in a curve of melon rind, upon which Elias had built a tiny pyre of straw.

His hand gleamed with albumen, very nearly baked opaque from the heat radiating off his skin, and he buried the yolks and shells in the frost-hardened soil. The chill air pawed at him, trying to steal down his throat with each breath, but the Flame danced defiantly, sending up little puffs of steam whenever the groundfog dared creep into the melon rind.

When he returned to his nest, Mother was already up and putting the kettles on the chimney cranes. She glanced incuriously at him and resumed her sleepy-eyed duties. By now the Flame had consumed all of its straw, already smaller, barely the size of Elias's thumb. He grabbed a pinch of moss from the woodpile, which it greedily devoured, before he made a more durable pyre of shards and splinters.

Elias realized the Flame was constantly hungry. Away from its home, a messenger of great and portentous confidence, assaulted on all sides by the bleak, chill hokum of Elias's world, it fought for each breath, each word.

He built a mighty fire in the hearth for the morning, earning a halfhearted scolding from Mother as she shoved the surplus logs to the side lest they scorch the coffee and porridge. Elias, however, minded not one whit. He sat cross-legged, melon rind in his lap, his seeping, charred hand tucked beneath his coveralls. He dropped bits and sundries into the rind, here a pile, there a path, watching as the Flame moved to consume them, obeying his whims.

The family was awake, fed, and out the door before Elias laid down next to the Flame. He was barely aware of their presence at the best of times, and now only relished their absence. Mother said something about his eyes, but she turned away when he looked at her, finding a sudden reason to perform some duties out back despite the morning chill.

A blink and a yawn, and then he devoted the fullness of his world to the Flame. He inhaled its heathen aroma, ever-changing as it consumed the different meals he sacrificed. Here, a stray bit of duck down, greasy and vivacious; there, a twisting of Tansy's auburn hair caught in the comb that Mother kept in her desk, sour and intrusive. The melon rind held a tiny lake of ash, shifting and swirling as the Flame scampered here and there. The rind itself was tough and pulpy; the Flame could find no purchase to scale its sides and escape.

"Now tell me," Elias crooned.

The Flame breathed life into the mysteries of the world, the austere truths that Elias knew must lay beyond the tiny clearing he'd once thought all of existence. He remembered being bothered by other small children at similar homesteads up and down the river, always running and screaming and prattling on. None of them wondered about the space behind their eyes, none of them wondered what it meant to live and die.

Elias heard the chiming words, felt the music of the Flame's canticles lift him up, but the language mocked him. The brilliant little spirit danced hypnotically, and Elias stifled another yawn, baring his teeth in a grim smile, jaw muscles aching.

"Tell me," he said, heart pounding.

Understanding flit like a mosquito in twilight, now close and buzzing maddeningly in his ears before vanishing. The Flame's chants grew faint, its movements slowing, all fuel consumed. Elias pinched a curled strip of wood from the pile and positioned it above the rind... before pausing. Considering.

"Tell me better!" he demanded.

The Flame bounced and leapt, shedding tiny impotent sparks. Elias waved the curl back and forth, the way he used to dangle a strip of pigskin above the dog, before the coyotes got her. The Flame's ethereal voice rose into a series of distant but clearly anguished squeals. It dimmed rhythmically, like the last beats of a failing heart.

"See? You can do it," Elias said encouragingly. He lowered the curl, raised it, grinned, and then dropped it into the rind. It burst into light immediately, coiling like a spring as the Flame devoured half in an instant before savoring the remainder.

Elias lay back down on the hearth, cradling the rind against his belly. He carefully lowered his burnt hand, tracing a finger around the ash, drawing nonsense designs and scooting the Flame here and there. The egg scabs cracked and seeped yellowish pus, but the pain was a distant, othered thing. "I brought you here for a reason," he said, pinching at the Flame's extremities and giggling at the flashes of heat. "I've been patient. So patient..."

The Flame hissed whenever his scorched nail passed through it. The whispers became cross, petulant, defiant.

"Tell me, and you can eat all you want," Elias promised. "I know where Mother's been squirreling the duckdown for winter muffs. I know where Father and Mason hide the gunpowder. Can you imagine that? You'd go off like firecrackers, you would. Pow!"

The Flame muttered, crawling back and forth on the dwindling curl of pine.

Footsteps crunched outside and Elias sighed, long and suffering. The Flame jigged and juddered in the gusts of the boy's breath. "Let's get," Elias muttered. "This is too Important."

He stole out the back with practiced ease, grabbing a tuft of brown yarn from Mother's sewing pile on the way. The Flame fed, sending up more twists of thready black smoke that stunk of lanolin. Someone called his name, but he was beyond such petty things, and no-one cared enough to pursue him.

"It's working already," he smiled, bringing the rind up to his nose. "Come on. I have such sights to show you."

Elias wandered the day away with his Flame, skirting the darkness just inside the woods and keeping well clear of his family. He showed it where his siblings had started building a treehouse, until Tansy had fallen. He showed it where Lucky and Bertrand were buried, on a rocky thrust just overlooking a muddy bend in the river. He showed it the river up close and personal, pretending to float the rind away before laughing and jerking it back into the air. A few floating specks of water batted the Flame around like a cat playing with a shrew, but Elias dropped in a few drying husks of grass to show there were no hard feelings.

Noonday came and went. Elias was starting to wish he'd gotten any sleep the night before; his ears felt cotton-stuffed, and he had to blink one eye at a time lest they grow too heavy. His stomach grumbled loudly, and even licking at the flaking egg on his blood-encrusted hand seemed tempting. But this was Important.

"Tell me," he started repeating, his own chant as the day became early evening. He hugged the rind to his chest, plucking random bits of nature and dropping it in without care. The Flame whispered, oh yes, better than before, *louder*, but there were so many other sounds out here. Even the ghostly wind through the boughs drowned out the Flame's words.

"Tell me, tell me, tell me," he sing-songed, trudging drunkenly towards the sounds of chopping wood. Through gaps in the trees he could just make out either Father or Mason stacking cordwood under the eaves. He didn't have long to wait before the dinner bell summoned them, leaving the yard empty save for the last mindless clucks from the chicken run.

Moving on deerstalker's feet, Elias made his way up to the cabin. He filched some feed from the chicken bucket, not minding the sweetly sour film it left on his teeth. He grabbed one of the girls' scarves they'd left hung on a nail and wrapped it around his neck against the rapidly-descending chill. He balanced on Mother's chopping stool, stretching his good hand out and just managing to get his fingers under the unlit tin lantern, lifting it off its hook.

The sky was the red and purple of a deep hurt when he returned to the smothering embrace of elm and spruce. The Flame lit a haunting halo around him, giving the impression of countless inky creatures darting from branch to branch. He paused to admire the shadowy audience he'd created when he heard something new on the wind, loud and braying compared to the Flame's.

Mother called his name a few more times, and then, after tremendous silence, slammed the door shut.

"Alone now," Elias croaked, wishing he'd dunked his head in the coop's barrel. The rainbarrel would have been better, but it had been a dry, dry summer since Father had repaired it.

It was only a short distance to the aborted treehouse, but it felt like miles to his leaden legs. In the flickering light, the messy debris of sticks and planks and scrounged shingling nails rose like a long forgotten tower.

Elias sat with a thud, sloshing half the day's ash out of the rind and into his overalls. A cloud of it rose around his head, digging into his nose and his parched throat. He coughed and hacked but waved it away, desperate to make sure the Flame hadn't been snuffed in his carelessness. Sitting like the last candle holding out against Hogmanay, the Flame remained, faint and subdued.

"I can't wait any longer," Elias complained, not sure he was any louder than the Flame had been. "This is your last chance. You're going to tell me, and you're going to be loud… or we can't be friends anymore."

The Flame spat out a single tiny spark, which drifted into the ash and died.

Elias set the rind on the ground and laid the lantern in his lap. He'd never been allowed to refill the lanterns like the other children, or even use them; Father's face had gone queer whenever Elias had asked. When he was older, they said. When he was more careful, they said.

He laughed, a low sound like a hen burping up gravel. The lantern was mostly empty, but enough weight sloshed around to cause both himself and the Flame to brighten up. He fumbled with the tin cap, which stubbornly refused to turn no matter which way he twisted, until it spun free in his eggy fingers and flew off into the darkness. Warm, fishy odor spilled over him, making his tummy rumble.

He turned the lamp until the thin, viscous oil splashed onto his fingertips. He held his good hand up and flicked, tiny droplets bursting into brilliant white light where they struck the rind. The Flame screeched with joy, leaping from spatter to spatter, growing larger for a moment before receding. In seconds, the fuel had been consumed, but the Flame bounced energetically, eager for more.

"Speak up," Elias said. He spilled a little more into his palm and carefully poured it into the rind.

With a speed that shocked him, the Flame roared and expanded until the rind seemed a pitiful prison. Elias yanked his hand back but could feel a new burn rising along the edge of it. The Flame stood now, distinct and defiant, barely knee-high to the young boy but a far cry from its early form.

Elias's eyes sparkled. He threw back his head and laughed, hooting his joy to the tracers of flash-bang color that marred his vision. The Flame spoke now, singing, SCREAMING, true words and secret lies and buried incantations. Too soon, though, it receded, seeming to shrink into the distance rather than into the rapidly-crumbling melon rind.

"Yes! Yes!" Elias stammered, scampering to his feet. "I'm listening! I want to know it all! I want to know everything!"

He held the lantern over the Flame, tilting it carefully, oh so carefully, until a steady stream of droplets tumbled forth. Each one filled the Flame with a terrible white light, tinged with blue and so fierce as to make the back of Elias's skull ache if he stared into it. *When* he stared into it.

"Of course," he laughed, finally understanding. "Of course!"

Despite his bone-deep tiredness, he couldn't keep from dancing as the Flame finally told him everything he wanted to hear, confirmed what he suspected to be true. He shuffled back and forth, scuffing his dirty feet in the dry needles.

He settled and tilted the lantern forward again, and almost immediately nudged the rind with his toe, spilling the innervated Flame in a flood of ash. Elias cried out, reaching dizzily for the Flame with his cracked hand and overbalancing, landing hard on one knee. The lantern swung on its handle and cracked against his jaw, jerking back and spilling forth a great gout of oil.

The Flame roared, a cacophonous eruption like the grandfather of all thunderstorms. Elias shut his eyes against the searing light, but it found other ways in. A heat that numbed crawled up his nose, over his ears, soaking into the scarf and tightening around his throat. He hurled himself backwards, throwing the lantern with all his might and slapping furiously at his face.

The Flame's sweet, succoring words were gone. All Elias heard now was a bellow of triumph, of mirth at the unfettered freedom and destruction, and derisive laughter at the foolish little boy who thought himself capable of containing it.

When he finally pulled the scalding scarf free and managed to open one cracked, oozing eye, he found the world around him burning. Streaks and slashes, like the lines of God's own pen, crackled with lantern-bright flame in wild patterns. A path of smouldering needles followed Elias as he crawled backwards on all fours, the stink of whaleflesh painting the inside of his mouth.

The Flame, twice as big as a man, stalked away from him, deeper into the darkening wood on lightning bolt legs. Waves of fire spread out in a wake behind it, climbing tree trunks and setting even the soggy black spruce alight.

"Come back here!" Elias tried to say, but nothing came out. Even if it had, he was dimly aware that he could only barely hear the sappy greenwood crackling and popping around him. "You come BACK!"

Hands slapped at the remaining spatters of burning whale oil that stained his overalls. Elias was jerked into the air, hot breath on his face as Mother and Father screamed soundlessly at him. Over their shoulders, the Flame danced joyously, spreading its knowledge with the whole world.

Elias cried the whole way back to the cabin, that final mocking laugh echoing in what remained of his ears.

***

27 Years Later

Their little corner of the muddy river valley had recovered, more or less. They say half the North burned that year, but of course that was just foolish fancy and exaggeration. It had been a goodly portion, no doubt. The Great Cariboo had been closed for months, re-opening just in time for the first snow.

The locals were fond of telling just how the trees at Trilby Home had grown back, though, and even more fond of telling how they'd looked the days and weeks after the Great Fire. It were like an arrow, they'd said, two lines, just as straight as you please, pointing directly at that little mud-daub log cabin, a mighty black wedge of destruction that only God above could truly appreciate. The cabin had survived, praise be... but weren't that strange, too? Half the North burned, a hundred homesteads lost, and didn't it just seem like the fire had just popped over to Trilby Home to say hi-hello?

Nearly three decades on, the all-but-abandoned Trilby Home had finally reverted to the bank. The gold rush was over, the rail rush was on, and lumbering hadn't yet returned to the savagely burnt areas of the region. Elias didn't know if one day a man in a fancy suit was going to walk up to the Dutch door off the empty coop and try to kick him off his family plot, but he knew he had ammunition aplenty should the need arise.

Summer had stretched long this year. Hot and dry all day and only getting down to bearably warm and smothering at night. Waves of smoke rolled through the valley, but they were distant, sterile things, smogging up the sky and reddening the sun. The last of the horse was keeping the stewpot and Elias's belly company, but after that it would be hardtack and salt trout until he could come up hunting again.

Today, though, the smoke was hot, sharp and dirty. Brown tides smeared the horizon, darkening the late afternoon almost to twilight as they swallowed the sun. Elias ran his good palm over his bald, scarred head. Only a few patches of hair had survived that night, and what grew in was white and wispy.

He stood straight, inhaling that familiar, vibrant stench. A new light reflected in his eyes, blooming to the west as it crested the hill. He'd known today would be the day, sure enough as if he'd been counting down the Christmas advent calendars with his brothers and sisters. For days now he'd woken up with laughter in his ears, familiar and cloying and scornful, but it always faded until his world returned to its familiar still silence.

It didn't fade today.

The great fire roared down the hill, tree crowns exploding like matchsticks, driven by the furious easterly winds. Sparks swirled around Elias like flies on a corpse, gusts of kiln-heated wind sending his ghostly clumps of hair flapping like hanging moss.

The Flame laughed, as true and real a sound as Elias had heard in many a year, and Elias laughed back.

"Tell me," he croaked, spreading his arms wide to embrace his old friend. He stepped off the crumbling porch and walked, proud and steadily, into the smoke-choked woods.

"Tell me."

FIRE SEASON

By Michele Rule

Wind wafts smoke through window
prompting me to rise
slam it shut.
Ash sifts silently and settles.
The sky grows smoky in the west.

Rust orange glow.
Fire has taken hold
out of control
threatening homes.
Owners have fled
important things
hastily packed.
Pets
Paperwork
Computers
Where is that list when you really need it
Medications
Clothes
Time to run
unprepared.
Only what you wear
not even shoes.

You sit
frantically scrolling the news
a single scrap of good

or even bad
better than
silence
as you wait
for smoke to clear
flames to falter
find out
what is left
of home.

PERCEPTIONS OF DESIRE

By Asha Jade Goodwin

I won't say I was the first person to see a Blaze, but I will say I saw them a week before they were shown on the news. Go look up my interview – you'll find my quote. "The fire moved with intent, like a person," was my testimonial. "My eyes were red and my lungs seized with exhaustion as I choked on the smoke that danced with the fire."

Actually, could you pass me a water before we start? My throat's a little dry. Yours too? Thanks. I feel like I can always taste the smoke, even indoors. Where were we? Oh, right.

Of course I didn't mention that they looked like women, with curved hips and beautiful, flickering locks of hair. I didn't think anyone would believe what I saw. I didn't believe it myself.

No, I don't like the term "fire-nymphs," and I refuse to use it. The only thing they are fucking is the air quality. Okay, sure, there have been more than a few people who were apparently so overcome by lust that they ran into a Blaze's arms, but is that really the Blaze's fault? It's like calling an angler-fish an angler-nymph – have you heard what happens to the males of that species? Look it up. Maybe we should be calling them angler-flame's instead; that would be a more apt description. No, I don't think fire-siren's makes sense, because I have never heard them sing. Fire-maidens? Fine, let's agree to disagree. You and all your listeners can call them fire-maidens and pretend there is no threat.

Yeah, no, I wouldn't call myself a regular listener. Sorry. Oh, of course, if someone sends me a segment that intrigues me I always listen, but I'm not a subscriber.

No, actually, not everyone who sees them in person is overcome by desire and dashes into their arms, "going out in a blaze." How do I know? Because I saw them! And, after taking a moment to consider what I was seeing and then promptly dismissing it as some sort of hallucination, I ran the other way. Attraction? Nothing to do with it. I love women! Are you saying you'd fling yourself into the arms of a Blaze if it looked your way?

You have a poll? Oh. Wow. Those numbers are alarming.

Look, let's move on from the apparent fuckability of fire and instead discuss what they are and where they came from. As far as I know, as well as not being overcome with lust at the sight of them, I am the only person who has seen where they came from, and I'm here to release my statement.

It was a tower of living flame.

I was hiking a trail alone when the scent of smoke wafted past my nose. I turned towards it, and I could see this great column of fire, descending to the ground like some angel from the Bible. I stared at the flame, and I felt as if it were staring back at me; I was sure that I was hallucinating and began to wonder if my brother had stuck something extra into my water bottle.

And then the flame twisted and from it sprung seven figures.

Yes, those ones were feminine in shape, just like the rest that are burning our forests.

No, I didn't think about how beautiful they were, nor was I overcome with the want to dive into their embrace. I thought, "Oh shit, I need to get out of here." Because even if I was hallucinating women made of fire, I could still feel the heat and smell the smoke, and everywhere they stepped was bursting into flame.

What do I think is the point of them? I'm actually so glad you asked. See, I have a working idea that maybe – well, I don't know if they've always existed, or just spontaneously sprouted, but I think how they interact with the world might clarify and change our perceptions of other supposedly mythical creatures. Say, as you brought up before, sirens. They are said to lure men and drown them. But what if they weren't meant for men at all? What if their nature is simply to fix or correct something that is out of balance? Or even feed on it? And for the sirens that was fishing, or the ocean biome, or maybe something else utterly unknowable. And a side effect is that maybe men tended to find them attractive and drown. Maybe it wasn't intentional.

Well, I do think the Blazes are doing something important. They are clearing away the underbrush that we've fought so hard to keep from burning, making way for new growth. Or maybe they are feeding on it – I don't know the physiology of these things, and I don't think anyone alive does. Maybe some of those people that chased after them into the forest got intimate enough to find out, but unfortunately their charred remains don't speak.

Maybe we need to equip one of those people who answered "Yes" in your earlier poll with a camera and some sort of fire-proof condom to find out. No, wait, I'm not actually suggesting that. Can we cut that part?

Do I think we can fight them? I'm going to be honest with you, I don't think we can. Who knows what the final equation of desire and death will be? At this point, for our safety, we should probably just leave them alone. Let them feast; hopefully we can rebuild in the fertile ground they leave behind.

We should also think about what other areas of the world we've been suppressing nature violently, and what we could change before the next "siren" appears.

Because if we go with the "feed on what's out of balance" theory, I'm betting against chastity.

West Kelowna Burns

By Jaki Sawyer

This mid August morning
my attention jerks from glittering lake
to ominous pewter billow
boiling northwest over clouds and hill
memories uncoil

Base not visible, we would have said
two-way radio crackling *column rising high*
head office calling for helicopters
Initial Attack Crew
into the air in five minutes flat

No need to see flame
I already know wildfire
its hungry roar
lung-choking odors
ash that grits your teeth
that you cough up
days later
eyes stinging red
exhaustion

but still I look up
as if I expect a chopper to land
unload the grimed and weary crew
and wonder
do I have enough bread, soup made

how many pork chops thawed
what else can I prepare
for sweat and smoke-stained firefighters
even the chopper
thud of landing
sounds exhausted
old faces grim
young faces
decades older
than they were this morning

RETURN

BY ALEXANDER ROBERTSON

Li pressed her head against the window, the vibrations pulsing through her skull, blurring her vision as the blackened landscape flashed past.

"You ok back there, hun?"

Li grunted in reply.

Mom didn't press for more. Li watched through the vibrating reflection as Mom turned around to stare out the window too. Dad had been silent for hours. He only got like that when he didn't know what to say, and that was rare. Li missed his indomitable positivity, even if she had once hated it. It was different now. It seemed the fire had burned away so much more than just trees and houses. It had burned her family, even though they'd escaped the flames.

And even though the flames were long gone, the smoke and ash hung on the air, the sky still hued a faint orange. It wafted through the air filters and hung inside the car. It lingered. Somehow Li knew it would never truly leave. Even once the smoke blew away, the trees regrew and the houses were rebuilt, the signs would remain.

A black mark on a tree trunk, the crunch of melted glass underfoot, white of birch where fir once stood. Few would notice them, fewer still would care to think of the blaze that once had been.

They passed a blackened sign that had once proudly presented the name of their town. The town was gone now, just like its name. So many before it had gone the same way, far more still to come.

Li was happy to some degree, and she felt guilty for it. Mom and Dad had already decided they were moving. To the coast, to the cities. To somewhere the firefighters could protect. She'd always wanted to escape the tiny rural town, but she had never imagined it would be like this.

Dad drove slow through the town. Past the McKenzies, past the Daniels. They stood amongst the charred remains of their homes, holding each other, crying. Li knew she would be doing the same soon enough. It gave her some connection to them, the same shared connection of place she'd always been so keen to spurn, to escape. Watching them grieve their lives here; it somehow made her feel more at home than she ever had.

The car came to a stop in front of their block. Only the chimney remained. Mom was already crying when Li got out of the car. It felt like a dream, like it couldn't be real. With the protection of the car's filters now gone, the smoke stung her eyes and tore at her throat with each breath. Tears spilled from her eyes as she embraced Mom; partly from the smoke, mostly from her heart. Dad joined them and they mourned together in silence.

Mom broke away eventually, to pull a tissue from her purse and blow her nose. She offered tissues to the others, and Li dried her own tears.

Pushing down the soreness in her throat, rubbing her eyes red raw, Li walked over to the cinders. Her steps slow, lethargic, as though she were underwater. She bent down to touch the remains. They were cool enough now, belying the heat that once burned hot enough to melt the window frames.

She made her way through the rubble to where her room had once stood, where her books and magazines had sat on shelves, only to provide fuel and further the flames. It was in here somewhere. It had to be.

Rummaging amongst the ashes as tears ran down her cheeks, she found a small misshapen metal box.

Black ash covered her fingers as Li picked it up and dusted it off. She strained, unable to loosen the lid.

"Let me try," Dad said.

With his strong, weathered fingers, he pulled the lid free and handed the box back to her; the bent, dark metal was now decorated with overlapping fingerprints.

"Thanks," Li said.

Li quickly wiped her hands on her pants, then took out the bracelet tucked away inside the box. The one she had forgotten to grab when the evacuation order came in.

Blue and green yarn imperfectly woven around each other. A stray thread poked out, where it had once snagged on a bobby pin. Her and Ellie's initials marked metal beads; woven between clay imprinted with memories. Li slipped it over her wrist and leant into the embrace of her father.

A reminder of all she had lost was all she had found.

UNRELENTING

By Raegan Cote

smoke — smoke — smoke
smoke
headlights
road
road — pylon cone — road
  blue eyes
  you —

breathe
decade old
remnants
of northern BC
coniferous
turned ash
& plummet
toward my chest
like a boulder
dislodged
from soil.

i lay
under
your fire
trap body
as your hands
grip my lungs
& control air

flow
  in
  & out
  you
  & me.

look at
our skyless sky
through backseat
windows
smell rain
& dampen
your urgent escape
from me.

Frogging Hour

By Em Van Moore

146   RED EYES AND TIRED LUNGS

Rocks on the dirt road lit up like creatures in the headlights. The car bounced and shadows moved, bringing the rocks to life. Adam used to drive white-knuckle on the steering wheel, dodging and weaving to avoid frogs and toads as they went to and fro from one side of the road to the other. Bugs used to swarm too, smearing on windshields and coating lights.

Now, nothing lay before the car except the crowding of dusty trees and an empty, desolate dirt road beneath an inky black sky.

Adam turned down the street to his house. He pulled into the driveway and sat for a moment.

The world was silent. At least the miasma of spring wildfire smoke hadn't started yet, ruining the yard and the view of the Nechako river beyond. It had been the whole reason they'd bought their house in the first place. Back when they were newlyweds, it was easier to imagine things improving, that mankind would get its collective shit together in time to mitigate the worst of the crisis.

He sighed and emerged to cross the threshold from the outside world to his home.

It's easy to forget sometimes that things weren't always this way. Life used to be noisy; so loud it was deafening, the roar a comfort. Without it, the quiet was even louder. No more so than the quiet between himself and his wife, Evelyn. He hoped she would speak to him tonight.

He went down the steps into the underground house. "Hey Evie," he said, tossing his bag on the table near the door. He kicked off his shoes and joined her on the couch.

She shifted over to make room for him; a good sign, in his experience. After a tense moment she relaxed and lay her head on his shoulder. "How was work?"

Adam sighed, relief loosening his body. He leaned into her, wanting to kiss her forehead but stopping short. He turned his mouth away instead. "That salmon farm has been having a banger spring," he replied, "almost five thousand already."

"That's good news. What's the water levels like today?"

He had to hold in another relieved sigh. She hadn't asked him about work in weeks, after a nasty fight about the future of the planet. She'd wanted to have kids years ago and he had refused. Sure, when they'd gotten married he was more optimistic. But now, with the world the way it was, he'd changed his mind, and he didn't feel like it was her place to change it back for him. "Water levels are almost okay. Nearly enough snowfall this winter, but without the glaciers..."

It was her turn to sigh. She tensed, undoubtedly expecting him to remind her that one good winter and one good spring didn't mean anything was worth being hopeful about. That's what he would usually do: try to bring her back down to earth. Not the earth as it used to be, but the earth as it *was*.

That night, he didn't. He just put his arm around her shoulders and gently pulled her closer, until he felt her relax against him once again. "How was your day?" he asked quietly.

Evelyn snorted. "I can't get Aiden to stop biting! None of my positive reinforcement works, he just really, really likes to bite. Never had a student so focused on eating others like he is."

"What about a doggy chew toy?"

She snorted again, this time with an accompanying laugh. He'd missed her laugh. "I don't think his parents would appreciate that."

"Well you're the expert, not them. They have three kids, you have thirty. If you think a chew toy would help…"

"I don't," she replied good-naturedly, "but thanks for the suggestion."

They settled into a comfortable silence, and though Adam tried to focus on the TV show, he couldn't. Evelyn was warm next to him, her weight on his side, her head tilted back against his arm. The silence between them had been hostile for weeks, but something about seeing the clear, smokeless sky had soothed his frustrations, making him more pliable.

Plants lined the walls on rows of thick shelving built into the cob. Skylights bordered by metal grating offered views of the starless sky above. The house hummed, alive in its own way.

The last forest fire had been extinguished the previous fall. It had been preceded by one of the best summers in decades. Only a few tens of thousands of hectares burned, and though they came close, they never threatened. Their city had been spared since being rebuilt a half a century prior. Each winter the town celebrated "City Planners Day," a long weekend to toast the three people in all of northern British Columbia who actually planned ahead for the worsening climate crisis. After the city was leveled by fire, they'd lobbied and petitioned until they got their way.

A new urban landscape emerged.

Underground houses with shutters and self-sustaining filtration systems. A family could live for weeks below the earth, safe from the forward march of fires above.

A city that was as beautiful as it was functional. Water catchment reservoirs on each building fed into pipes that would spray the structures down, preventing them from errant sparks and flames. Parks with recycled material playgrounds, restaurants with farms on the roofs, and a town center that doubled as a bunker – all carved marble and secret stores of food and water.

Even the forests themselves had been redesigned, populated with poplar and fire-resistant plants who begrudged catching the flames that came their way.

But that didn't stop the smoke from the surrounding towns. And it didn't stop the inevitable march of environmental change. The frogs disappeared. And the bugs. It was hard to tell if they died out at the same time, but the croaking of amphibians was more noticeable than the absence of biting mosquitoes.

Sure, some remained. Last holdouts of already-doomed species. Smoke resilient deer. Urban bears. Squirrels who changed from eating food scavenged to food dug up from the earth, tubers and roots previously favoured by other, long gone, animals.

Adam thought about the way his life had changed since his childhood, and how he missed the little comforts. Sleeping with the windows open in the summer, feeling the breeze on his face. Fishing for salmon in the fall, hauling twenty kilogram beasts from the raging Canadian rivers. Even cleaning the bugs off his headlights would have been a welcome annoyance, because it would have meant there were enough bugs to splatter all over them in the first place.

"What are you thinking about?" Evelyn asked. She tilted her head up to meet his eyes, the whites reflecting the tv screen.

"Bugs," he replied.

"Bugs?"

"Yeah."

"That's a weird thing to think about."

"I miss them."

She wrinkled her nose, a habit he'd always found precious. "You miss bugs?"

"Among other things."

Evelyn kissed his cheek and turned back to the tv show, her lips leaving warmth on his skin. "I'm sorry you're missing bugs and other things." Her barely audible voice betrayed her thoughts. She never did like to discuss dark topics, choosing to dismiss them or ignore them outright. Sometimes he wondered if she thought them at all, only to be reminded in some small way that she was as deep as the ocean and as accessible as the Marianna's Trench. Of course he knew, especially when they fought about children, or the world, but when she gave him the silent treatment it was almost a welcome reprieve from having to talk some sense into her.

He used to want to plumb her depths, hear every thought in her head. But he'd given up years ago, settling into a pleasant domestic life of affection and distance. It was hard to get too attached, even to your own spouse. A hurricane could take them. Or bury you in a mudslide. Or a plague could wipe you both out, leaving non-existent children behind.

Better to love them at arm's length, where they were safe from the heart wrenching loss of your passing, and you were safe from theirs.

The lights flickered and went out with the rest of the power. The battery powered emergency lights blinked on a second later.

Evelyn sat up, her body illuminated. "Crap. It's been cloudy for weeks... I can't believe I forgot to check the levels!"

There were limits to their self-sufficiency. Sometimes things just ran out of juice, and they'd live by the light of the ceiling windows until the solar cells recharged. It was the job of the first person home each day to check the levels and this time it was Evelyn's turn. It had been Adam's the day before, and he'd forgotten too. Clearly they'd both been slacking.

"I'll go do it," Adam said. He knew Evelyn hated the dark and the unknown of whatever was hidden out of sight in the yard.

"Are you sure?" she asked quietly. "It's my fault..."

"It's fine. I need air anyway."

Her smile glowed in the dim light of the backup system.

Adam threw on his coat and shoes, then ascended the steps to outside. Once on the clover lawn he stopped and took a deep breath, enjoying the feel of air traveling down his throat to his lungs.

At the utility bunker near the carport he opened the hatch and climbed down the ladder. There was an underground tunnel he could have taken, but they'd filled it with boxes and furniture. The systems had lulled them into a false sense of security by not failing for over a year. In fact, he hadn't needed to repair anything since two summers prior, when hail had shattered seven of the ten 'shatterproof' solar panels.

It took less than ten minutes to get everything switched over to auxiliary power, drawing on a buried propane tank they'd gotten installed out of necessity when they built the homestead. Sure, they could have sprung for the high-end systems connected to the house so they'd never have to leave it at all. But the mini honeycomb of rooms accessible through tunnels was how they'd both been raised, in the halcyon days of the old world when people were still trying to figure out how to survive the climate crisis. It was comforting, in an inconvenient way.

Climbing back up the ladder to the world above, Adam thought about his home and how alien it might seem to people a century before. How his own grandparents might have looked at it in wonder, marveling in its subterranean efficiency. Like an earthship below ground, it was alive, needing constant tending and maintaining. They'd built it by hand, like most people did after the fires razed their previous homes.

At the top of the ladder he shut the hatch and swatted at something that buzzed away.

The clouds opened up, droplets falling onto the tin roof of the carport with rhythmic clinks and plops. The familiar fear of rain gripped him, spurring him to a run. He thought he felt his skin tingling, his hair and scalp burning. He hadn't bothered with a jacket for the quick excursion to the utility bunker, so his short-sleeved shirt slowly soaked through from the shoulders down.

Adam wiped drops of water from his face as he ran, and then stopped short near the front staircase. His eyes weren't stinging like usual. His head didn't sear with pain. He tasted the droplets, and they were cool and clear. There was no acid or chemical rain forecasted. He froze, his foot on the top step leading down to the house.

Rain fell harder, gushing from the sky to shake the branches of bushes and trees, patter off anything hard in a cacophony of noise. He turned his head up, letting it wash over his face. A coyote howled in the distance, its voice carrying over the forests. An answering cry returned its call.

The world was alive once again, loud and raucous.

A sharp prick jabbed at Adams bare shoulder, and he slapped at it unconsciously. When he pulled his hand back he was mildly surprised to find a small smear of blood and black insect body on his palm.

Something moved nearby, shaking the stalks of early season tulips barely poking out of the ground. His heart leapt. He stepped back, eyes scanning for a threat.

A black shape hopped from the flowers with a wet splash on the clovers. Slimy skin, bulging eyes, and four little wriggling legs. It looked up at him, eyes inky black.

He looked down at it, his breath held in his lungs.

They both remained frozen for a few seconds, each assessing the other. Strangers in the world, but united by survival.

And then Adam watched as it squirmed and hopped off to the yard beyond to disappear into the untamed forest bordering their lawn. He hadn't had time to trim it yet, clear all the weeds and fire starter. The frog was swallowed up by the shadows of that underbrush.

Something moved in the dirt driveway to the other side of him. He exhaled his deep breath and waited. Another frog squelched from the bushes and across the drive to a puddle where it sat and stared for long seconds.

Adam remembered how the country used to be when he was a child, and how the amphibians would become very active each night around a certain time. They'd cross from one side of the road to the other, going somewhere he never understood. If there was a storm brewing they'd be even more active, hopping along in the headlights of the vehicles to be crushed beneath their wheels.

As an adult, Adam had always avoided them, dodging and weaving to keep from slaughtering the little creatures. *'The Frogging Hour'* his parents had called it, blaming the activity on changes in barometric pressure.

It hadn't been that time in years, the animals dying off or disappearing to other, more hospitable, ecosystems.

The frog in the puddle stared, as if daring him to get in his car and go for a drive. How many would he see on the road if he did?

Something small and sharp bit his forearm. He slapped it.

When he looked at his palm he found a similar smear to the one from his shoulder: black insect body and a bit of red blood. He never thought there would be a day when he'd be glad to be pestered by mosquitoes, but after a long absence they were welcome visitors to the outside world.

Adam considered that he may have been wrong when he kept trying to bring Evelyn back to reality about children. Perhaps it was he who was living in a world which didn't exist anymore, one of hopelessness and despair, and she was right about them being in a new one after all.

The frog on the driveway started calling, the sound distinct among the falling raindrops.

Despite himself, Adam smiled. Normally he would hate to be wrong, but in this case it felt good. It felt right. It felt like hope, for the first time in a very, very long time.

The Frogging Hour had returned.

Haikus from a Midnight Morning

by Asha Jade Goodwin

the sun never rose
midnight sky at eight a.m.
smoke chokes the city

burnt deep orange sky
made dark by death, ashes fall
coats my car, my lungs

darker still at ten
night lights can't illuminate
summer forest fires

on wind ash floats by
the smoke tracked inside like mud
with sun, sky is grey.

THEY CALLED US MONSTERS

BY DREA LAJ

Each soot-filled breath sears my lungs as I choke down fiery air, chest heaving, heart thumping, blood boiling.

Flames chased us, bone-tired, from the mountains, through the valley, and to the sands emerging from the ocean. They silenced our anguished howls as we vowed never again to be chased from our home. But the ancient grudge sparked, leaping and tearing through our sanctuary once more. A fire storm driven by hatred and unstoppable ignorance.

The roar of the flames signals the end. The past is immutable and refuses to be consumed. The crimson sky blots out the moon and the land flushes red. Tonight, those responsible for the flames will pay. It ends with me.

***

We congregate in a mossy clearing, our last refuge from those who sought to cage us, conquer us, or worse. Laughter crests like the distant surf as a dozen families socialize around the communal fire.

Already the moon's energy fans my nerves. My eyes meet Rafe's dilated pupils over the flames as the sun dips below the mountains. Though this night is only my second change, tradition dictates and circumstance demands my parents secure my future by my third moon. If I am to be wed, he is my mate. Our lives – past, present, and future – merge here in this field.

His smile saturates me in his inferno and sanctuary. We snap together like feral jaws before gliding in unison towards the clearing's boundary. Alone.

His soft fingers stroke my bare shoulder before traversing my sundress's strap on their way to my neck. I tilt my head to grant him access as he strokes the side of my throat.

"We only have moments until the moonrise, Ione." His warm brown eyes bore his animal passion for me.

"I sense it."

His laugh rumbles in his chest. "What else are you sensing?" His fingers trace down my spine, counting vertebrae.

I gasp as he tickles the small of my back. "The night. Your fingers. You."

"Have you thought about what the night means? What it means to give yourself to the pack? To me?" He pulls me closer. I surrender to his embrace. My eyes cast towards the fire. Earlier, I'd tossed my college acceptance letter into it. My double-life is over. Our numbers are dwindling, so my aspirations of college are forfeit in duty to my people. Rafe confirmed his duty at the last gathering.

"No more books." I surrendered myself to this decision.

His left hand strokes my chin and tips my face up, and his smile forecasts many exuberant children. "First, our responsibilities." Rafe traces my jaw and I lean into him. "Then ... everything you desire. I want you. Claim me tonight. I promise to honour your dreams."

My sacrifice's reason is unspoken – women carry the wolf gene. Choosing a wolf mate increases our chances but does not guarantee them. Yellow flecks overtake the brown in his eyes.

I interlace my fingers in his. "You are my choice." Ceremony or not, Rafe is mine. I've loved him since I learned what love is. His love is quiet, patient, and steadfast.

Emboldened with my consent, he leads me towards the thicket. I stop. The flickering city lights to the south threatens our peace. But at this moment, our freedom is secure. Unburdened, the young ones sing and dance as grandparents prepare their sleeping bags. Their coming slumber will be peaceful under the watchful eyes of the pack. May they never know what it means to be hunted.

My parents pause their preparations to wave, granting Rafe and I their blessing. My hand in his, we disappear into the trees.

Hot, dry forest air deadens the laughter from the clearing. The campfire is extinguished. The moon will rise and will be one under her splendour.

My dress slides from my shoulders and pools among the desiccated leaves and twigs at my feet. His eyes wash over me. The bonding ritual requires a deep, unifying connection. He chuckles before unbuttoning his cotton shirt and removing his pants.

I close the distance. But something prevents me from caressing his bare chest—an unnatural sound in the forest. Silence.

Then the world explodes into a deafening rage. All red and yellow and black as heat hurls us back.

Without thought, I careen towards the orange flame barrier separating me from my kin. Rafe grabs my shoulders, keeping me back. The shouts of men rise above the inferno.

Hunters.

"There's nothing we can do. Here." Rafe thrusts fabric – my sundress – into my hand. "You'll need it."

"What will you do?"

The flames find purchase on tinder-dry trees and claw skywards. Black smoke chokes life from the once-vibrant copse as the acrid smell burns my nostrils.

Rafe is silent.

My hand grips his. "You can't. Come with me."

Crack. Venerated firs tumble as the flames consume them, fueling the destruction.

He squeezes my hand as sparks explode around us. "I'm sorry. I love you, Ione. Always."

"I love you, too." My chest aflame, not from the singed air but from my heart breaking. If losing my dream hurts, losing Rafe guts me. Black, billowing smoke blots out the moon. The hunters will advance until they capture or kill us all. Our only hope is to transform and evade the inferno and the hunters by blending in with the other animals.

His fingers slip from mine. "Go. I'll be right behind you. I promise."

A lie. His duty is to the pack. Mine is to escape. Our birthright lives – or dies – with me.

***

Rage boils beneath my skin. They called us monsters. Be careful what you wish for.

A handful of us remain untouched by flames and steel. Our eyes meet. Cousins. Grandparents. Children. So few left. Our backs against the cliffs that separate the sky from the ocean and the blaze and hunters at our fronts, our options are limited.

They thought they could wipe us out, relegating us to the stuff of legends. Not tonight. We will fight to survive and see another day, another chance to stop the destruction with those willing to listen to reason, instead of fear.

The moon summits the mountain. Her light red with wrath. Energy crackles, setting my nerves ablaze. Fur ripples down my arms. I howl. My kin mirrors my resolve as the humans take their position against us.

I am vengeance. I am destruction. We will be free.

August 17, 2023

By Rod Raglin

Tonight the wind is blowing
and I'm thinking of fire
flaring, leaping, exploding
jumping roads and breaks
raining cinders
billowing, blinding, choking smoke
I'm thinking of leaving everything behind
except my life and loved ones
a convoy of vehicles
snaking out of town
stalled on the highway
an arena as a home
worry and tedium my companions
tonight as the wind blows
and the dry lightning flashes
I'm thinking about fire
as my future
I'm thinking we waited too long
all that's left to do is evacuate

BURNING EYES

By Payne Haynes

Tizzy was in a tizzy when Charles found her. He watched from afar for a bit as she screamed at a fireman. No one seemed to pay her any mind, which only made her even more angry. She was athletic in that *I-worked-my-farm-all-my-life* way and wasn't about to be ignored. It wasn't until she kicked an empty metal bucket that they seemed to respond. Satisfied with their reaction, the woman stormed back to her farmhouse mere feet away.

Charles followed her in and stood in the doorway as she moved around. She glared at him as she passed with large round eyes, reaching to fetch something from the pantry. The itch was so intense she was forced to rub her eyes. It left her cursing as she returned with no dry goods.

"Eyes okay?" He asked. His voice was surprisingly mild for his size.

She glared at him. "Ever since the wildfires! Why aren't they doing anything out there? And what is with those damn birds; they shouldn't be here with the fires?"

"The ravens? They're just doing their bit," he said.

"What kind of bit is that?"

"Guiding the lost."

She tried to fill a pot with water, yet there was no water. Another curse left her lips. "What is wrong with these people? They turned off the water while there are fires?"

"Perhaps there is something you're not seeing going on?"

"Like what?" She demanded as she turned to face him. "My whole family went to ensure the fire didn't reach the house. They will need a hot meal when they get back and I can't even get enough water to boil?"

"Your family is okay."

"How do you know?"

"I walked up the road and saw them talking to some firemen."

Tizzy rolled her eyes and opened the fridge to pull something out; it was empty. "What the fuck?" she screamed. "I just bought groceries! Where are they?"

Charles did nothing to stop her from pacing and raging. He just watched from the doorway. He waited as she slammed the appliance closed and opened the cupboard. Again, there was no food on the shelves.

Finally, in the pinnacle of rage, she stood in the middle of her kitchen and turned to face him. "Did the firemen take it all?"

"Would that make sense? For them to clear out the food when they're fighting fires?"

His tone did not settle her mood. She turned away from his calm logic and opened the freezer.

What was in there was not food. It seemed to swirl of darkness and stars, and teeth? Before she could fully examine the horror that was her freezer, a long stride carried Charles quickly across the room. With a powerful hand he slammed it shut.

"Now would be a good time to calm yourself," he said, in a strange voice that bore obedience.

The horrors had chilled Tizzy. She silently sat down at the kitchen table. "What was that?"

"That was something that would gladly feast upon your anger," he said as he leaned against the freezer. His back ensured the door wouldn't open again.

Tizzy hugged herself as she forced herself to breathe. "Nothing feels right. Just..."

"Now that you're not so upset, you're becoming a bit more aware of things."

She nodded silently. "I'm sorry I yelled. I've never seen ravens behave like that. And the firemen ignored me. I hate being ignored."

Charles said nothing. His body bounced a little as a powerful attempt to open the freezer door hit him. He didn't seem to mind; instead, he waited for her to think things over and make the realizations herself.

She stood up and looked out the window. The firemen were no longer fighting fire. They seemed to be regrouping and talking. A few pointed towards the house while others pointed the other way. "Where is the fire now?"

"It passed."

"Passed? It can't just pass." Her voice was small as if something was slowly dawning upon her. She spun to face him, "Am I dead?"

He said nothing. When she glared at him accusingly, he nodded towards the mirror on the wall where neither of them appeared. A cry came but was stifled in her throat. "I... I stayed to make dinner. Keep the house safe."

"The ravens cannot guide you until you are ready. Are you ready?"

"No. I can't leave, not yet." She told him. "My family."

"Shall we go see them?" he asked. "We could just walk up the road and look."

He stepped away from the fridge and offered her his arm. Tizzy hesitated; it was surreal. Yet his arm was firm and gave some comfort. They walked outside and past the firemen. No one paid them any mind.

She paused as they reached the driveway and turned back. Her breathe hitched as she saw not her farmhouse but rubble. The firemen were not planning; they were going through the rubble and putting out the embers of her home, her grave.

She clung to Charles's arms as he continued to walk with her. Down the long driveway they saw a barricade. Her father and two brothers were there. They were broken down into tears on the side of the road as firemen comforted them. Even the firemen looked upset.

Her father, an elderly man, looked up and saw her. It was hard to see him clearly as smoke rolled around Charles and Tizzy. Her eyes burned and her lungs felt tired as she gave him a warm smile. She didn't want him to worry. It wasn't clear if he saw it before the smoke thickened.

Her father watched as the smoke rolled away, looking for signs of his daughter he just saw. She had been standing there with a man, smiling back at him. He was sure of it. The smoke cleared away, but he didn't see anyone. All he could see as the smoke cleared was a large owl, sitting and watching him with large, familiar eyes.

Smoke Choked Skies

By Asha Jade Goodwin

What do the woodland creatures think-
This darkened morning with no rain?
Oh, can they smell this awful stink
When they draw breath, does it cause pain?

Perhaps they left already, east
Where can the fires never go?
Somewhere that fire burns trees the least
Maybe the land of ice and snow

What do the city people think
This smoke-choked morning with no sun?
Under the ashen sky they sink
Soot-filled lungs, nowhere to run.

Untended lands left to rot
Consequences considered not.

What World is This?

by Cherie Hanson

I n 2003 a fire engulfed the sky over several subdivisions in the town where I live. It was new to us, news to us. Our town, stretching along a section of the lake's 135 Kilometres of shoreline, had never before experienced the ferocity of flames burning trees to the ground and sweeping through neighbourhoods. We watched as the fire was buffeted along by its own created winds and weather system. It invaded the very airspace.

After the inferno, there were photographs of dark silhouettes standing blackly against the red and orange flames. Pictures were printed in national newspapers. It was an extraordinarily dramatic event. The charred bricks of fireplaces stood jaggedly, surviving where houses once stood.

We were still so naïve back then. We believed that it was an anomaly, a freak event. But our high desert arid conditions continued year after year. We were at times shrouded in poison ladened smoke which drifted over the town. At first, we didn't take it personally. It wasn't an Okanagan fire. It flowed toward us from the Cariboo, or Chilcotin. Even further afield, the grey tinged yellow smolder would settle on the top of a local mountain or settle on the street where I lived. The houses across my street were veiled from view.

In 2009, several fires burned relentlessly in the province. People packed themselves up and became refugees while fire fighters fought to save what they could. This was shocking, the sudden explosion of flames driving people from their homes. Those fleeing the danger were stunned that their homes were so vulnerable. We were, protected and living a predictable life. Everything was planned and secure. We counted on it.

Right on the heels of the summer blazes in 2009, the summer of 2010 saw evacuations in four areas of the province. We were beginning to fear the trees that stood around our houses. We were anxious about the forests pushing into the subdivisions. The shelter of trees and shade desired in past years had become a worry.

In 2014, five areas covering thousands of hectares flared again. The Red Deer Creek fire crossed the border and invaded Alberta. Fire knew no boundaries.

2017 brought the worst wildfire season on record up to that time. The air was tainted. People complained that they could taste the bitter death of trees on their tongues. Their eyes were red with particulates of trees and soot. People were exhausted from the toxins that crept into the houses through cracks, window frames, under doors. They had tired lungs, swollen sinuses, throbbing throats. Some complained of their voices shutting down, a loss of range, a strange reedy sound when they talked.

Records were broken again in 2018. The estimate area engaged in fire was 1,400,000 hectares. But the public was beginning to understand. At first, Kelowna held a marathon when the fires were filling the air. Gradually, the realization that particulates could create long term lung damage began to become common knowledge. Fewer people were out hiking with their children to keep them healthy.

The summer of 2023, a long sweltering time with little rain, lead to 1,818 wildfires burning across the province.

On two different occasions I stood with my neighbours on the sidewalk in front of my 1946 built house watching fire creep over Knox Mountain. Trees went up like flares. The flames moved like northern lights, dancing, diminishing, then flaring again. Both threats were extinguished.

Our little village of neighbourhood people gathered at a small park on August 15th to watch the McDougall Creek Fire burning across the lake. We were confident the lake was protection and there was no threat to our homes. Surely the ash and cinders could not jump the lake. Water extinguishes fire.

By August 17th we were caught up in horrific fascination as the wall of fire descended the brow of the hill across from us. It was powerful, swift, and relentless. We watched the red and yellow wall attack the forest and the neighbourhoods.

We watched while the spiraling grey smoke of fire landed on the shore, we were so sure was safe. Several fires broke out in neighbourhoods behind our local, now reddened, Knox Mountain. The previous rescues had left the hill stained.

The challenges were multi-layered. Would the fires sweep down and destroy our war time bungalows? How much risk were we taking by simply going out the door? Would our future be one of lung disease and shortened life span?

By now, we knew what fire meant to our lives. We had been on alert for evacuation in past fire incidents. We knew how to pack our cars. But the question was where could we go that was safe? Where could we go without the flames reflected red in our eyes? Where could we go without the aching lungs and physical exhaustion of tainted air?

We had somehow landed on a new planet. How long could we count on it to sustain human life?

TEN LITTLE NOMADS

BY LILY AUTUMN WEST

Katie fled the choking smoke which cremated her home,
  Made camp with others dispossessed, united they would roam.
  Ten little nomads in a catastrophic world,
  All condemned to nature's fortune, except the final girl.

Derek's tummy took a turn that shut his systems down,
In flora laced listeria, he writhed upon the ground.
Ten little travellers went out to dine,
Derek got the poisoning, and then there were nine.

They said Alice took barbiturates to fill her empty belly.
But some suspected jealousy in Sam's girl, Shelley.
Nine little scalawags stayed up very late,
But Alice couldn't rouse herself and then there were eight.

Andrew smelled a rotter; he didn't trust their tale.
He let the clan go on ahead, climbing hill and dale.
Eight little lowlifes camped in wooded heaven,
Andrew wouldn't leave the grove and then there were seven.

Mark the hemophiliac broadly notched his thigh,
And without a surgeon's tourniquet, shed ruby woodland dye.
Seven little litterbugs, chopping wood for sticks,
Mark slipped and cut himself and then there were six.

Dave received the short straw, crawling in to get supplies.
The crumbling rafters boxed him in, an unpleasant surprise.
Six little looters, scouring a dive,
Dave vanished in the rubble and then there were five.

Amy followed Dave to hell, resolved to tow him out,
The flame-wracked structure supped on her ere she could loose
a shout.
Five little mourners settling a score,
Amy fell below the cellar and then there were four.

Shelley always heeded Sam when he made poor decisions,
'Til she pitched into the rapids with most of the provisions.
Four little mariners stumbled on the sea,
The waters swallowed Shelley and then there were three.

Miller punished Sam when he tried to ravish Katie,
Throwing cliffside jabs and uppercuts in honour of the lady.
Three little vagrants fought like creatures in a zoo,
Miller fought a man-bear and then there were two.

Sam peered down the cliffside, sought the man with whom he
tangled,
But hands below wrapped 'round his legs, so both men dangled.
Two little wrestlers waiting for the sun,
Sam lost his footing in the dark and then there was one.

One little nomad left all alone;
Katie grabbed the duffel bag and wandered on her own.

SUGAR JUICE

By Lily Autumn West

194   RED EYES AND TIRED LUNGS

My town was smothered under summer flames. In winter the floods came to rewrite the maps again.

Trailer park villages slid into the Fraser. Highways, bridges, hopes and dreams, all swallowed up by the unchecked waters.

Empires collapse when infrastructure fails, and the Pacific Northwest was no exception. We knew the climate would come to collect one day. It was quick and violent, severing the Coast from the Interior.

Help wasn't coming. Smoke signals are no good when the air tastes of fire.

There were only two seasons now: smoke and flood. In smoke season, the clouds burned and your lungs filled with ochre haze. In flood season, your flame-touched shelters were dashed against the riverbanks.

We were drowned in flames and engulfed in water.

Sam was right about one thing. You had to keep moving to survive.

At first, there were ten of us. And then there was one. One brown-eyed girl, standing on a mountaintop, singing 'til my lungs screamed.

The nine have faded into wispy memories. But I've tiptoed through the outskirts of the hilltop town that rests at the base of the valley. Trudged on foot to Spence's Bridge, seen Lytton plunge into the Fraser. In all that time, I haven't seen another soul.

When the first drops of inky rain fell, I found the Oasis. It was a roadhouse diner on a gravel lot overgrown with sage. I remember stepping over the sign – peeling turquoise and hot pink on splintered ply. No power, no water, no front door. But it had a roof and four walls to house me. I curled up in the big corner booth for six and slept soundly on the torn red vinyl.

Like most of the canyon, the Oasis had been evacuated in a hurry. I avoided the fridges and freezer – God knows I didn't want to find some long-forgotten hamburger. But there was a wood paneled Coke machine with six yellowing buttons spread over two rows. And I just knew there was some sugar juice inside.

That's what my dad used to call it. Sugar juice.

My eyes watered, but it wasn't the haze. The machine reminded me of every road trip I'd taken with my dad, driving up the canyon from Vancouver to Prince. You'd suck in your breath on the hairpin turns, praying there wasn't a long hauler over the yellow line; pass the time holding cold sugar juice in your mouth until it grew warm and stopped fizzing.

I'd had boyfriends who swore the drive took two days. Dad did it in eight hours. With me, he did it in ten. We'd find some roadhouse gas station on the side of oblivion, with cheap sandwiches that smelled of fry oil and a raspy waitress who called everyone Hun. There were never any guardrails. I was always scared that a truck rumbling by would shake our car off the parking lot and it would plunge into the depths of the canyon.

We'd always get a can of sugar juice. We never told mom.

The red and white machine was layered with inflation stickers – the latest read $1.25. I didn't have change, but the sugar juice dispenser didn't have power either. A hammer behind the counter made short work of the lock. But it chipped the wood paneling. And I couldn't explain why that made me uneasy.

The prize was mine. But a little voice in my head said:

"Nobody wants a warm Coke, Katie."

When you're half-starved and totally alone, calories matter. Instant mashed potatoes and fry oil supplemented the occasional unlucky marmot roasting over smouldering furniture. It wasn't sustainable.

I had already smashed my way in. I could have grabbed a can and chilled it in the mud. Instead, I found a glass that lived expectantly on the counter. My sugar juice would be served with ice cubes.

The generator was out of fuel, but its very existence made me believe the machine could thrum to life again. I craved the happy clink of coins disappearing and the satisfying ka-chunk of a cold can deposited at my feet. Digging in the booths produced three quarters. I carefully placed these in the cheeky jar that read, "If you fear change, leave it here!"

I should have just opened it and moved on.

But sometimes we choose sanity over survival.

That sugar juice machine gave me hope in the deluge. Every morning, I'd wake up and see the red, white, and brown. And every night, I'd kneel at the shrine to my youth and tenderly rub soot off the Formica. To me, it was the canyon before the landslides turned boomtowns into ghost towns.

Fire season came faster and hotter than I remembered.

My long stay had consumed the Oasis from within. My corner booth bed, the counter, and the sugar juice dispenser were the only survivors. Everything combustible had been sacrificed to keep me warm. I'd bled my wintering roadhouse dry... except for the machine.

I was out of time. I felt the torched air on my skin. Saw the ash tumbling by my doorstep riding on vicious winds. Heart pounding, I knelt one last time next to the sugar juice machine. This was it. I choked on the thick air through my bandana. Opened my backpack, closed my eyes and pulled the two-layer door open.

It was empty.

Not a single can.
I couldn't understand.

The fire was moving fast, the heat of the flames getting closer with every panicked breath I took. I pushed the shrine door closed. I couldn't bear to see it like this. Hands shaking, I slipped my quarters into the coin slot, and the sugar juice machine rejected me, returning them one after another. I could barely hear the clinking of betrayal over the roar of the wildfire outside.

There was nothing left for me here. Feeling very, very foolish, I turned to face the flames that filled the sky.

The Earth Is Breaking Up with Me

By Cherie Hanson

I lay on my pillow like a 14-year-old,
not understanding why
the boyfriend is slowly shutting down.
He no longer smiles when I walk out my door.
He has become inconstant in his moods and
unpredictably fickle.

Among the conflagrations of flaming summer, I cry
my eyes a swollen red.
The mutilated words shut down my throat.
There is nothing I can say.
Eruptions of anger taking a revenge.

I remember when the hillsides were more seasonably
likely.
Now, I fear that which I once embraced.
The treed slopes are a menace waiting to attack.

My throat is red.
My lungs are more tired with every breath.
And like the young girl,
I know nothing can be undone
once the breaking up has begun.
It is a timely pouring out of grief.

BEAST

By Cassidy Muir

It lumbers its way through the lodgepole pines, brushing the brittle green needles from the branches; the rusted ones crunch and snap, a carpet of orange and brown under its massive feet. The songs of whiskey jacks, robins, larks, and warblers, the chittering of squirrels and droning creak of high branches, deaden at the sound of its uneven, shambling gait.

Each breath it pulls in is an agonizing, wet rattle. The viscous black fluid filling its lungs drips from its maw and coats its paws. The steady dribble leaves a trail behind it in the litter of needles, evidence of the miles it has walked with no rest, no sleep, no water. The rough bark snags its coarse hair, ripping it out by the roots. The beast does not notice. Its massive heart pumps like a coal train engine, smoke billowing out of its dry, cracked nose in mechanical puffs. The hot, stagnant air becomes filled with the sound of hacking and sucking, the smell of rotten decay.

Fur clings to it in ragged, greasy clumps. Ticks, ants, and beetles crawl among the knots and mats, finding shade from the sun in the valleys between its ribs and the knobs of its spine. Horseflies pick at its open sores. Black flies gorge themselves on the remains of rotting meat and fruit stuck between its teeth. It surely must be in agony, but it does not, or cannot, cry out in anguish. One clumsy foot in front of the other, step by step, it marches on, and on, and on. There is no telling its direction. There is no purpose. There is no destination.

It leaves silence in its wake until the towering pines stop swaying, until the smoke rises into the ether and the ragged breathing fades into silence with distance. Gradually, the chorus of birds picks up once again. The arid stillness resumes.

All is almost as it was.

SOMETHING GOOD

By Kilmeny MacMichael

208   RED EYES AND TIRED LUNGS

What is something good that happened to you
recently?

Sweet jambusters and toast these questions get
harder
and harder to bear

Meeting you was
but meeting you as soon as I get in, drag off my suit
give myself a bit of a scratch, too sweaty yet
for the full advantage of a shower

It's hot out there and the atmosphere keeps blowing
fuses
threatens to leave us all in the dark
it's hard to match your grin

Would you be quite so chirpy and eager to pepper all
comers
with conversations
borrowed from that imbecile on the talk-tablet
if the filters stopped pushing the air clear

If you had to breathe the burning
of the livescapes you once played in
felt the ashes of memory weigh down your lungs
and scorpion your eyes

because you forgot the decade and lifted your goggles
wiped away a tear of frustration at this scouring
world
would you be smiling if you had to go out there?

Something good you want to hear about, you
safe and cool in your dim cocoon
you should tell me
something good and what have you done to your hair
what colour is this why striped like a skunk
you've never seen one not even at the side of a road
bloating and stinking

We keep you sheltered from all of that
within these walls
you stare at your screen instead and who can blame
you for
following it far away
with its colours like green and music like whale stars
its imagined existences
beyond all possibility
you tell me any technology sufficiently advanced
seems like magic

You believe in magic or I do
magic that will one day make it safe for you
to go outside
without my sacrifice my red eyes and tired lungs

I do not have to see the shadow behind your smile
crying and yelling alone of course I know
but what more can I do

Do you think my stories of racoons stealing
the ears of corn in grandmother's garden
chimerical, fairytale?

What is something good that happened to you
recently?

You are something good that happened that happens

You the future
the future a sparkling a shine
an allegiance that one day

We will after all come out
be above
get to the far side
live beyond promised

No longer content ourselves with surviving
but radiate prosper shine
get that taste that
make ourselves that
something good that happened
it's happening.

Hearts Aflame

By Jonathan Riggs

The sun hung above, an angry red spot in a grey sky. The ever-present haze of the burning world turned the yellow star into a bloody wound in the smoky heavens. Searching for one glimpse of blue, I found nothing but smoke. Another dreary day fated to fade into a night without stars.

I sighed and pulled my eyes from the sky, scanning the forest that stretched out before me. To the east, the blight bloomed. A wall of red and orange, a sickly mockery of autumn colours. A gust of wind rushed through the branches, swirling the dead leaves from their perches to discard them carelessly on the forest floor. Sweeping past the still-living green forest, my eyes settled on the west. The sea of green came to an abrupt stop at the Bluebeam River, where the Vuroso Wasteland lay beyond. Grey, black, and brown was all there was to see, and a shiver ran up my spine at the thought of being in a land where the only trees were burnt husks, stubbornly refusing to fall into ash.

As I turned away from the waste, I gazed upon green forest. Tall tree-formed homes stretched far above the canopy of the forest, futilely attempting to reach beyond the ever-present haze.

I placed my hand on the trunk of the Denav tree I stood in. I felt the life surging through the tree. No sense of blight or insect disrupted the flow of energy passing through the hardened bark. Relief flooded me for a moment, yet anxiety filled me for the tree I had made my home in; the tree that I had planted when I was finally of age to understand my responsibility to the forest. Blood and sap were bound together when the tiny Denav seed was placed gently into the dirt. It was the tradition of the Goedil, the tenders of the trees. We were raised in the forest, bound to its fate, caring for it until we were laid to rest at our tree's roots.

I couldn't remember the last time I saw another of the Goedil tending the forest and I feared that I was the last.

The blight weighed heavy on my mind as I walked through the woods, moving steadily toward the diseased trees. The smell of decay struck me as I drew closer, the familiar autumn scent so out of place in the heat of the early summer. I frowned, touching the closest tree, searching for any sign of sickness. My stomach churned as I felt invasive insects gnashing through the wood. I withdrew my hand immediately. Bile rose in my throat as I fought the urge to vomit. The violence of the beetles consuming the wood and the sorrow of the tree as it died from the inside out burned in my mind. Hardening my heart, I placed my hand on the tree and drew its energy into myself. Cracking and splintering, the once healthy wood decayed by a decade in an instant. I withdrew my hand and quickly moved to safety.

The weakened base of the tree exploded into slivers of dry wood and the tree collapsed to the forest floor.

I looked sadly at the remains of the gentle giant. Reluctantly, I stepped toward the next tree.

A sudden cracking of branches startled me. I whirled to see a rush of fur and feline features streaking toward me. Not taking a moment to consider my path, I set off into the forest at a sprint.

My pace was terrible. With lungs that were achingly weak, I gasped for air as I dodged around trees and leapt over protruding roots. Low-hanging branches and jutting sticks tore at my green flesh as I ran, drawing blood that urged my pursuer forward with greater urgency.

The puffing of the creature behind me began to fade, but I didn't slow or look back, unwilling to take my eyes off the path ahead. Images of myself sprawling flat over a root and allowing the beast to leap on my back spurred me onward. Wheezing, I burst through a small bush and found no trees ahead. The ground dropped away, and I rolled down the embankment, finding myself knee-deep in the Bluebeam River.

I froze for only a moment as the cool water rushed around my legs, rejuvenating me. My lungs no longer ached, and I could feel my wounds closing. Remembering my hunter, I rose, sloshing noisily through the water, white foam surging around my legs as I forced them forward.

The river grew shallow again, water falling once more to my knees, then my ankles before releasing me to scramble up the embankment. The thought of claws shredding the flesh of my back and hot, fetid breath being the last sensations before my life ended pushed me up the steep slope hurriedly.

Spinning quickly at the top, unable to stand not knowing how far death was from me, I was shocked to see empty forest with no cat in sight.

I stood dumbly, watching the bushes I had emerged from for any sign of movement, scanning higher in the trees for a potential ambush. As I debated what to do, the creature that had chased me came into view.

It dragged itself from the bushes, claws extended into the ground, pulling itself forward. Its breath came in ragged gasps that wrenched at my heart. Its fur was patchy and there were several gouges and partially healed wounds on its flank. It was desperate to feed. It drew closer to the embankment and tumbled down, crashing into the water. Its maw struggled to break the surface, water splashing onto the banks as it was dragged by the current. Its claws raked the water. Wide, fearful eyes gazed up at me.

I turned away.

The grey wasteland of the Vuroso greeted me. Treeless and hazy, particles of ash blew into my face. I coughed, trying to rid myself of the invading particulate. My chest tightened and I gasped between bouts of coughing fits. Tears streamed down my cheeks as the smoke in the air burned my eyes. I fell forward, lightheaded, my vision swirling. My hand sunk through a soft layer of ash, settling on the scorched earth below.

I felt the pleading of the soil below, begging for new life. Begging for renewal.

I channeled my power into the earth, even as my coughing caused stars in my vision. The nutrients eagerly took to the life I offered it, and a sapling sprang up through the ash, reaching six months of growth in an instant.

I crawled through the ash, heeding the call of the soil three more times before I dragged myself to the bank of the river. Rolling down the steep embankment, I splashed back into the water, letting it revive me. The cat had been pulled out of sight by the current, its body claimed by the water to feed the fish. I drew deep breaths, grateful for the clean air and the aid of the water in my quick recovery.

I looked once more at my saplings, lonely green sprouts in a plain of ash. I smiled at them; my heart full. I spent the evening fantasizing about re-growing the dead lands across the river. In my dreams, I wandered the world covering forests like my father had before me.

***

Trips across the river to plant new saplings became part of my daily routine. The air began clearing along the bank as the power that kept the smoke and ash from floating into my forest began to take effect in the new copse.

Green grass spreading from trees to the riverbank caught my eye. I looked around slowly, admiring my work when a sudden movement caught my eye. My heart stopped in my chest as a figure lurched about the base of my new trees.

One of the Vuroso had found my trees.

Long grey hair hung down its face in tangles. Mottled grey and black skin covered the emaciated frame. It stood at the base of one of my trees, reaching a trembling hand forward. I watched in horror as the hand rested upon the bark of the tree. Remembering tales of Vuroso burning forests and seizing Goedil to burn them alive, I stepped back, causing a few stones to clatter noisily into the water below. It spun toward me, and I raised my hands to ward it off. To my surprise, the creature turned and attempted to flee.

It collapsed to the ground after a few steps. I watched a creature that I had been raised to fear and felt only pity. Standing silent, watching as the Vuroso dragged itself forward to try and escape me, I resolved to help it.

It looked up from where it was dragging itself, its eyes widening in terror as I drew closer. I noticed that the Vuroso was a woman; she looked to be close to death. Her spine protruded and her skin was stretched tight over her ribs; a cage holding her spirit in her failing body. Her black eyes widened as she tried to move away from me. I felt a pang in my heart as I watched her hand tremble, scratching at the ash, trying to find purchase.

"I won't hurt you," I said, my voice hoarse from disuse. She stirred the ash on the ground, causing it to puff into the air with her gasping breaths. I raced across the river, gathering dry branches and leaves. Carefully holding them above the water, I returned to the Vuroso, gently placing the offering in front of her. She reached out and quickly grasped onto a stick the length of my arm. I winced as the stick burst into flame.

I had heard of the power of the Vuroso but had never seen it with my own eyes. I comforted myself in the knowledge that the branch had been long dead.

The branch burned easily, turning into ash in her hand, falling on the already soot-strewn ground. She moved through the pile I had brought, the flames coming quicker each time.

I turned away to give her space, moving through the trees to check them and plant the new saplings. When I had no power left for the ground, I returned to her and found her sitting up and gazing at the trees. "I tend these trees every day. If you are here tomorrow, I will bring more to you." Attempting a friendly smile, I looked down and caught a glimmer of gold in her otherwise black eyes. When she failed to reply, I made my way across the Bluebeam and to my home again.

My life continued, and bringing the forest litter to her became part of my routine. The copse on the Vuroso side of the bank was becoming a small forest now.

As the Vuroso woman grew stronger, her black and grey skin began showing lines of dark red. Attempts at conversation were silently rebuffed, but when her strength recovered enough, she began following me through the new forest.

After a few weeks, the lines of red had become thick, vivid stripes, glowing a deep orange and bright red. Her hair had also taken on stripes of the same colours, the grey completely vanished, and it seemed to move as if always in a breeze. Her eyes were now a vibrant gold, the black almost completely gone. Her body had grown stronger with each day. Muscles that had withered returned to full strength and her bones no longer protruded from her skin. Her recovery and the growth of the forest had gone hand in hand.

My anxiety at having a creature of flame in such vulnerable woodland was dulled by the look of wonder on her face when she walked under the canopy. I looked forward to my time across the river, feeling the hope of the trees growing untainted there.

The blight moved further despite my best efforts. I destroyed more trees every day. I feared that the blight would never slow.

I woke one morning to the sound of wood splintering and groaning. Rushing from my bed, I watched as the tallest of the great tree houses leaned. Leaves fell like rain, caught by the wind and dancing through their descent to the ground. The wrenching of the wood hurt my ears as it creaked.

A mighty crack resounded through the woods and the tree fell.

The sound of trees falling became a daily occurrence from that point as the blight moved beyond my control. As more great homes succumbed to the blight, I knew then that I was the last of the Goedil.

The scope of my work in my woods shrank drastically. I covered the area surrounding my tree and no further. Each day brought the cacophony of crashing trees and the forward movement of the yellowed leaves. My planting increased in the land of the Vuroso, drawing from my body until I was nearly stumbling home. My silent companion looked on, her eyes searching mine, an unasked question behind her gaze. There had been a tension between us, an unspeakable subject that neither broached.

***

Walking the familiar paths, long trodden through the woods, I felt a desperate scratching in my mind. The pleading of my tree as the blight took hold.

I raced to the base of my tree, breath ragged and body on the verge of collapse. Placing my hands on the bark, I could feel the blight moving through, insects gnashing, bringing disease in on their filthy bodies. I screamed, flooding what remaining power I had left into the tree.

I couldn't help my tree fight the blight.

Sap filled holes and tried to push the insects out but wasn't fast enough to stop the spread. I tasted blood in my mouth as I continued to try and force my drained body to give its strength to the tree. I collapsed, hands still on the tree, unable to stand any longer.

I lost consciousness, waking later in darkness under a starless sky. I reached out and felt my tree quietly submitting to its fate.

I wept under the yellowing leaves, unable to collect the strength to stand. I cried until my throat was raw. The wind moved through the branches above me. I heard the leaves whispering, dancing, unaware that they were dead. My tree was fading, drifting quietly into oblivion.

I spent two days under my tree, feeling its life growing weaker. Its presence, once a comfort in my mind, becoming hollow and quiet. I wanted to sink into the earth at its roots, but I knew that I would provide nothing for the tree.

Despair washed over me in waves, and I wept intermittently until my body could no longer cry. I felt alone, adrift on a river with no one to stop me from being swept away.

***

I neglected the Vuroso for days, but finally remembered she needed the forest refuse. The idea of my tree's mighty branches falling and being collected to fuel the Vuroso caused a sharp pang of grief in my chest. Listlessly, I wandered the forest, collecting debris to bring across, loading my arms to make up for my time away.

When I arrived on the shore, I found that the Vuroso was not sitting waiting for me like she normally was. She was on her feet, a look of immense sadness on her face. Placing the wood down at her feet, I followed as she slowly pointed toward the trees. I felt dizzy bracing for new horrors. I reached out to the trees.

The blight had jumped the river.

My new forest was dying.

I clenched my fists as I moved through the trees, sensing the spectre of death hanging above the young canopy. I kept moving, hoping that I would discover any tree that still fought. When I found none, I fell back against the nearest tree, sliding down. My back scraped against the rough bark and my blood and the sap of the tree mingled as I stared at the ground.

The blight moved as though it were conscious, reaching its fingers of pestilence across the Bluebeam to grasp any source of life available. It seemed to have watched and waited for a single gap in my defenses and then struck. I had been out manoeuvred.

Red feet disrupted my view of the ground. I looked up slowly to see the Vuroso staring down at me.

Her face seemed to reflect my own. Golden eyes welled up with tears, tears that evaporated before they could fall. The question in her eyes, the looks that I had not understood finally made sense.

"Yes," I said, my voice coming out as a whisper.

She nodded once, turning to the trees and raising both of her arms; her fingers outstretched, she pointed toward the trees. I quickly scrambled away, watching from a safe distance. A deep red glow from her chest began to emanate before flames burst forth from her hands, eagerly devouring the ailing wood. Flames greedily raced up the trunk, spreading into the branches, devouring leaves. The fire roared as it did in my nightmares.

She burned my stand to the ground. The crack of branches and crash of trunks collapsing pounded against my ears as it was charred to ash before my eyes. As I stood looking at the still glowing remnants of my work, the Vuroso walked toward the river. She turned to look at me, her face holding a kind smile.

"Together," she said in a soft voice that held the echoing of cracking embers.

"Together," I affirmed as I followed her.

Pausing at the bank, her smile faltered, a look of terror crossing her face. I stepped into the water, holding my hand out to her. She hesitated briefly before taking her first step. A rush of steam hissed from the water and she screamed wordlessly. She grasped my hand, scorching my skin at her touch. Steam followed her steps as we moved through knee-deep water. She grasped my arm, hanging onto it with both hands as we reached the halfway point. Sensing she was close to collapsing, I lifted her arm over my shoulder, supporting her weight as her feet dragged. I could feel my flesh burning as we crossed, but I gritted my teeth and moved forward. Minutes felt like hours before I reached the other side, helping the Vuroso onto the rocks away from the water. Fetching wood, I looked down as she lay exhausted, her legs the same black colour they were when we first met. My wounds ached, already scarring thanks to the strength I drew from the water as we crossed, but the marks would remain.

When she had recovered, we moved down the familiar path, dread growing with each step toward my fading friend. When we reached the copse my tree resided in, I watched her stare in open-mouthed wonder at the towering tree before her. The trunk was thicker than she had seen in my small stand, its height and breadth utterly alien to her.

"This is your home?" She asked, looking at the stairs leading up into the boughs of the tree.

"It is my oldest friend," I said sadly, "It is my tree." I patted the bark, the once electric connection a flicker as it weakly acknowledged me.

"Stand back," she said lifting her arms toward my tree.

I retreated, hearing the roar of her flames. Tears flowed freely and sobs racked my chest. Waves of heat beat against my back as I blinked at the dirt. Smoke flowed into my lungs, aching in an already sore chest. I waited for the bond to break, for me to be truly alone, but felt nothing.

I braved a look behind me, seeing that the trees nearby were in flames. Smoke billowed from the pile of ashes that were once a towering tree. I felt numb as I saw the hole it left in the forest. The Vuroso rooted through the ash as the wind swirled it around her, making her a bright red glow in the storm of grey ash.

"Come, Goedil. See what our power once was," she called through ruin. I approached, ash drying my mouth and invading my nose. She was pointing at the ground, smiling warmly. I followed her finger, seeing a small seed resting in the ground, unhurt by the fire. "We weren't always destroyers. The Denav only releases its seeds with the touch of fire."

"Renewal," I said softly, scooping the seed into my hand.

"It's time for you to go," she said, reluctance in her voice, "We both have work to do." The fires were leaping from tree-to-tree, racing along a ground covered in decades of dry, dead growth.

She led me to the river through the smoke, my lungs desperate for the clean air again. I held the seed tightly in my hand, afraid of losing it in the inferno that was springing up around me.

"I'll need help tending to the forest," I said, stepping into the water's edge and looking back at her. "Together?"

"Together, Goedil." She said, smiling as she placed her hand on my cheek gently. I felt the heat of her touch, but my skin was not burning. "Until we meet again."

She disappeared back into the woods, flames springing up around her, her body burning white hot. I drew from the river while crossing, my body filled with power. A strip of green grass grew with my footsteps; the carpet that would one day welcome the Vuroso back again. The nutrients in the ground sang to me as I walked, plants and grass growing in my steps as I let life flow unhindered from me.

I found a spot for the seed, placing it gently into the earth again. I looked around, seeing vibrant green growth springing up and moving West. I looked East to my home, a bright blaze of orange fire casting heat outward, stopped by the river. I watched my home become ash but felt my heart aflame with hope for the future. Smoke rose from the sick lands that I grew up in, but I no longer felt their loss.

Stooping, I gathered a stone, the first for the bridge that would cross the river and bring the Vuroso back to me.

Vancouver Future

By Anneliese Schultz

Eyes fixed, straight up, on east-moving altocumulus
we hitch a summer's dizzy ride
feet curled and anchored, savouring sand.

Westward, broken rays of gold
begin to waterfall through huddled cirrostratus
to backlight hemlock
and then the yellowing larch.

In time, the red/black tankers and your
cruise ships like so much floating Lego
every SUV or Smart
will all be gone.

There will be only this polished stone,
the feather overlaying shell,
just unnamed clouds that shadow grey-charred
hillside
and then tuck themselves again
between the silent everlasting peaks.

Only these waves
precisely as it began
imprinting night across the soft cold sand ~

PARCHED

By Asha Jade Goodwin

This morning started like any other day: you woke up, showered, brushed your teeth (because you always skip breakfast), got dressed (because if you put on your shirt first, you'd get toothpaste on it), brushed the ash off your car, and drove to work with a throat as parched as the city's soil.

There should be blue skies with wispy white clouds above; instead, you can't even see the sky. You're sure it's still up there – surely there would have been some sort of emergency broadcast alert if it wasn't – but you can't even see a crack of it, just a thickening blanket of ugly, suffocating grey that seems to stretch on unending. Even the sun, orange and third-trimester pregnant, waddles languidly through the haze – so muted that it does not hurt to look at.

You stare out the window that frames your coworker's cubicle. It gives a perfect view of the smoke pit; astonishingly enough, there are people using it. At first it baffles you – how can they possibly stand to breathe in that choking air? Is it possible to be inoculated against smoke? Should we all take up smoking so that the terrible air, a future certainty, doesn't bother us? Your mind twists around the idea playfully, but the intrusive thought of asthmatic babies sours the joke.

On fresher days you'd take your lunch break outside, basking in the scents of burning rubber and grass. Today, outside doesn't exist. It reminds you of mediocre CG editing. If there was going to be a horror movie filmed in this town of yours, you think now would be a good time to do so. The ash floating in the air is eerie and reminds you of *Silent Hill,* or perhaps *The Mist. The Dreamcatcher* was filmed in your town decades ago, so why not another?

Your work didn't even bother with air purifiers this year – or maybe they upgraded the filtration system because the smoke is admittedly less dense inside than outside. But there is still a prickling stench permeating the building, and as the day wears on your throat grows raspy and grated, and a headache crowds your thoughts. No amount of water you drink seems to make either better; even the water tastes metallic and gritty on your parched tongue. Kitty-corner to your desk your coworker coughs violently and then lifts a puffer to her lips, gulping desperately. Blinking doesn't seem to moisten your eyes anymore.

Then your workday is done, and you are released into the world to enjoy your weekend, because it's summer, and shouldn't it be time for you to go to the lake and enjoy some sun? But one look at your phone shows a map with fires all around the city, telling you that no matter which direction you run, the smoke will follow. Instead, you drop your head and scramble outside. The smoke is in your hair now, you can smell it, and you know it will transfer to your pillow while you sleep. You slam the car door shut, a delicate trail of ash blowing in behind you; gratefully you suck in the stale air before starting your car.

You drive through roads that are foggy with smoke. Everyone moves a little slower than normal, as if the cars themselves have become sluggish with exhaustion. Peeking at other drivers reveals red eyes and pressed lips, nostrils flaring. Finally home, you gather your resolve and make a quick dash to the door.

This is the closest thing to a breath of fresh air you've had all day, which is terrible to say, since it's stuffy and the scent of smoke seems to be seared into your nostrils. Turning around, you check the seal on your door, then take a towel and stuff it against the bottom. In the winter, this is where a chilling draft slinks in. This summer, this is where smoke creeps in.

With your house successfully sealed against the smoke, you plug in the air purifier and set it to run at the highest setting. It chirps happily at you, flashing red for a moment and then blue as it begins to hum. Crossing to the kitchen you touch the tap to fill up your water bottle (for the third time today), but something large and black just outside the window causes you to jump and let out a surprised screech.

The round fuzz takes a moment to configure itself into a recognizable shape – it's a bear. An adorable, deadly, medium-sized black bear. You assume it's medium-sized because it's smaller than the black bear that battered your over-stuffed garbage can around like a soccer ball last week. Luckily the ratchet strap had held tight as you recorded from your window, helpless to stop if the bear had successfully pried it open.

This bear paces across your backyard – the only backyard in the area without dogs, so it has accidentally become a refuge for passing ursids if they manage not to be treed. You don't mind, much, other than the fact that you have to be extra diligent any time you step outdoors now. Not like you go outside very often anymore, not with all the smoke.

Besides, it's fascinating being so close to bears without any risk of harm, as long as you don't step outside. Like a reverse zoo.

Plus, they are adorable. You watch him sit down in the dirt; his mouth is slightly parted, and a long, pink tongue lolls out the side.

And those ears! How can something so deadly have such adorable ears? You take a picture and send it to your friend, saying "friend shaped," and she responds "I WANT PET." You aren't sure if she means she wants it as a pet, or to pet it, but either way you agree. Why didn't humans domesticate bears too?

Tapping on the window, the bear swings his head up in your direction but doesn't scuttle away. He's panting, biting at the grass that is patched brown like a worn quilt.

It stops being cute and starts being sad when you become aware again of the blanket of smoke; you can barely see the back of your neighbour's house through it. Your throat stings from sitting inside all day – how must the bear be feeling? He gets up, waddles out of sight. You move to a different window, tracking his movement, see him approaching your garbage can. Sighing, you watch as the inevitable happens. He swipes at the can, claws leaving trails across the plastic, then stands on his haunches to try and get into the top.

He works at it for a little while, knocking the garbage can over, dragging it away from your house. Annoyed, you think about how you'll have to retrieve it, and how you'll need to have a pair of gloves ready in case he does get inside.

But you can't fault the bear; his home is burning, and soon yours may too.

You already know intimately how these things can go; fifteen years ago, your childhood home went from still to ablaze in fifteen minutes. An hour later there was nothing left but cinders.

That time the community had rallied together, providing your family with food, water, lodging, and new clothes since the only things you had were what you'd worn that day. You'd been lucky – even as a teen, you'd taken to carrying your own birth certificate, your own SIN, your own IDs and money and bank cards. Your siblings weren't so lucky, nor were your parents, who had left all the important documents in a box in their closet. In a rural community, that had been a safe place to keep them – up until the moment your entire house was ablaze.

Of course, government documents can easily be replaced. It took time, but eventually everyone received their SINs and IDs and birth certificates again.

That wasn't the case for the childhood pictures and videos of all of your siblings from the pre-social media era. Nor your trophies, nor the WWII medals from your grandpa, nor the thousands of dollars in medical equipment for your grandma.

Nor the two cats, three guinea pigs, and iguana that had all been trapped in the house. No one was home to let them out. It had been a family day, taking grandma to the restaurant, loading up an oxygen tank for the excursion, the rest left at home.

The exploding oxygen tanks – and one particularly excitable tank rocketing out through an exterior wall – prevented the firefighters from safely entering the home. Instead they could only do damage control, which meant they kept the flames from spreading, but the house had to burn.

Now the fires press in closer to the city, and while no houses have caught on fire (yet) (in your city) (this year) (except maybe a regular old kitchen fire or something) there is still mounting anxiety. Yours? Or did it seep from all the denizens as they wait for a fate that feels inevitable, infecting you as well? If it does not happen this year, when?

In this environment, it is irresponsible not to have a go-bag ready. Yours is filled with all the things the government recommends: water, protein bars, a change of clothes, a first aid kit, a phone charger. You skipped the flashlight, because your phone has a flashlight, and didn't bother with a radio, because you have a car. Once upon a time the go-bag had been a joke with friends – everyone had the one prepper-lite friend, who "had a place" in case "it all went south." Fortunately, your friend did a good job prepping your group on how to pack the go-bag and had even bought everyone a backpack for it one Christmas. Unfortunately, their "place" was in the woods that were currently up in smoke.

Your bag had sat untended since the last season this smoky, and the protein bars had been so expired that even your friend who never notices expiry dates would have choked. The phone charger had been for an older model you no longer use. Now the backpack is updated, and it is at the front door, with your important documents ready on the kitchen counter.

Your grill sits outside, cover dusty with ash. This year you never had a reason to pull the cover off – every mildly clear day you worked, and every weekend was smoky. The propane tank is probably empty either way – you don't remember refilling it before the end of summer last year. It's easy to imagine that the whole thing has turned to rust underneath the cover. Easier still to not check. Time for macaroni again.

Exhausted, you fall asleep on the couch, only to be woken up hours later as your house rattles from a growling sky. Thunderstorms always comforted you, even as a child; their low rumble the rocking of your cradle. Even when lightning smashes overhead you are more awed than afraid, and you understand how older cultures believed there were gods in the sky, dueling over the fates of mortals. What fate will they assign you, you wonder? Hopefully not lightning upon dry grass in the middle of town. This August has been brutal for these dry thunderstorms, where the air, parched, crackles with electricity and the sparks alight on the already sun-burnt trees. Wildfires spring up in the wake of thunderstorms and thrive, wild and untamable, with no rain to wet their appetites. This thunderstorm will be no exception, and its nearness should terrify you, so close overhead that car alarms a street away have sounded; but the thunder is your lullaby, and you find yourself sucked into sleep once more. Perhaps your brain is too oxygen-deprived from a summer drinking smoke.

The next time you wake it is to a forgotten sound. A riotous, deafening sound – a million tiny marbles dropped across the floor and rolling, a tidal wave consuming the house. You sit up, alarmed, groggy brain not recognizing a sound that is heavier than you've ever heard it before.

Rain, like an ocean dropped from the sky at once, pouring down onto the parched land. You stumble outside, confronted by a wall of water descending from the eaves, and so enraptured you don't even realize that this is the freshest breath of air you've drank all summer since the smoke came pouring in from all sides. You take another step, bathed in the rain and instantly soaked, and then another. Through the pouring rain you can see other porch lights flickering on, silhouettes outlined in door frames; figures move into the street with heads tilted back and hands stretched up to the sky. Despite the hour, you aren't the only one to be lured outside by the sweet promise of petrichor.

The rain washes the ash from your red eyes, and your tired lungs fill with fresh air.

Long Wave

By Kilmeny MacMichael and
Asha Jade Goodwin

Red is one of the last colours to fade
in smoke or night
And tonight there is
only stars
neighbourhood dogs barking
evening birds clucking
waddling home
no movement on the mountainside
no deer
no flames
warmth trapped in the house

a mother warns a child
only ten minutes remaining
to play
to laugh
to watch one of the dogs
scratch its belly
with its back leg
between insistent messages

there is a breeze strong enough to ripple flags
shuffle the tiny flies which gather to suck the last
sweetness
from the continuously transplanted fruits of
summer
beneath trees shedding their shades

green to brown to yellow
and yes red

esthetic red
strawberry red ladybug red columbine red
crossbill red Mars red sanguinary or sanguine red
sunset ruby red

for a century people have swatted
these tiny flies away here
as if a few weeks makes a difference
before the frost fall ends them

let us write each other of happier things
such as
the sparrow who flutters deep into ever
green heavy seeded bush laden with next year
the water running strong carrying up n'tyxtix
(salmon)
returning home
the combustion tamed
and the poet who delights to write a song

let us banish red
until it is really needed
until it is all we have to see with
in the smothering star-winkle dark.

All the Help We Can Get

By Asha Jade Goodwin

The fire stalked her in two worlds.

In the night the winds had shifted. What should have been clear air upwind of the flames was now hazy, and ash coated the campgrounds. It didn't matter that it was four thirty in the morning – it shouldn't have been so dark. There was a stillness to the forest that hadn't been there when she'd collapsed into her sleeping bag.

"It's on the move?" Emma asked Andrew, her crew's Alpha leader.

"It's on the move," was his solemn and simple reply.

Breakfast was normally a frantic affair, scarfing cold Pop-Tarts and inspecting equipment, but today there was a heavy air on the camp. They'd cut through so much of the forest yesterday, sprayed down so many trees, but Emma knew that the fire was still spreading. This fire was barely fit for Initial Attack alone. They'd have to pull in a Unit Crew if it grew any larger. Her little squad of four hadn't been able to contain the fire so far.

Andrew was on his phone, marking directions on the app they used to strategize and track their efforts. Emma felt her feet dragging, but she wasn't about to waste energy yet. Mornings were hard on her – she was still stuck in that other world for the first hour until the memory of it faded, but today it seemed to cling to her stronger than ever.

Perhaps it was the ash in the air that pervaded both worlds that kept her mind stuck in the other.

Megan, the Bravo member of their team, and Owen, the Delta, were already packing up their sleeping bags. Emma moved to join them. Owen had dark circles underneath his eyes and his shoulders were tense. This was his first year in Initial Attack, and while his jokester demeanour jived well with the group when things were going well, he didn't seem to know how to act when things weren't. Emma counted down the seconds until he tried to crack a bad joke.

It was five seconds, apparently. "Wow, what a smoke show, eh?"

Megan rolled her eyes, and Emma was still out of it, so Owen's joke fell flat and he grew silent, pulling his gear together. He wiped at his brow with the back of his hand, smearing the dirt and ash there. Emma knew she looked no better – it had been their second night sleeping out here since the helicopter had dropped their overnight supplies and told them it wouldn't be able to fly them back yet. The one good thing about the smoke is that it helped mask the smell she was sure she was putting off.

"Grab your melons," Andrew told them, pocketing his phone. "We aren't leaving yet."

***

Emma had lived in two worlds her whole life. When she slept in one world, she'd wake up in the other, memories fading into dreams she used to tell her friends.

It seemed an act of providence when she'd learned that the BC Wildfire Service called their workers Wildland Firefighters. Wildlands was the name she'd always called her other home, the majestic world filled with magical creatures and impossible creations. When BCWS came to visit her high school last year, Emma knew immediately that she had to join.

Her first deployment came shortly after passing the WFX-FIT Test. She'd been the Delta on her crew, the junior member, bright-eyed and bushy-tailed – that was, until the moment she was face to face with the flames, hose in hand, wondering what the hell she'd been thinking as she sprayed the forest floor after spending hours cutting a trail and every muscle and bone in her body screamed at her.

And yet she'd survived that season and come back for a second. What had sent her back into the embrace of a forest on fire?

But now wildfires threatened both her homes.

In this world, Earth, she lived in a city called PG. Some years the fires would choke the skies until they were black with smoke for days or weeks; this year, a couple of fires had even broken out within city limits.

In Wildlands, she lived in Pauvrie, a bustling multi-tiered forest-scape that resembled treehouses designed by MC Escher, nestled against beautiful mountains. Everything had been perfect in Pauvrie – until the ash started to fall.

How no one saw the wildfire start baffled Emma – but she also knew that much like BC, Wildlands was filled with vast expanses uninhabited by sapient creatures. Magical creatures, sure, but not necessarily ones that could talk and warn others that danger was coming.

And now both her homes were threatened by the spreading flames.

In Wildlands, she'd fled with the rest when the massive wildfire rolled past her city, sprouting new fires in its wake. Those little flames had found purchase along the dry tinder that littered the forest floor and began to leap from home to home. Seeing the spreading flames had terrified her. She wasn't the same person there. On Earth, she always prided herself on being strong, much stronger than other women – she'd been one of only two women to pass the FIT test in her class last year. But Wildlands allowed her to be soft. Who needed muscles when a little magical dust could make all your boxes float? Why go on a daily jog when you could fly?

But Wildfire had brushed past Pauvrie, and Emma had run the other way.

***

Today they trekked along the same paths they cut with their Polaski's the day before, unwinding coils of hose behind them, one end connected to a pump from a nearby river. Their first job was to secure the perimeter of the fire – with the change in the wind direction, the fire could have spread in unexpected ways. Emma could see shimmering sparks in the ash-filled air. Her muscles ached but she kept trekking, third in line, focused on Megan's back, chopping wherever Andrew told her to, clearing brush that Andrew chainsawed. They arrived where they had left off the day before, the path immediately terminating into the underbrush. They continued to cut, veering their path to the right, following the new shape of the flames. With the movement of the fire, they needed to make sure there was a safe route out.

Emma couldn't even see the sun through the thick haze that filled the forest. Time had no meaning for her during these days. It was easier to lose track of it, lose herself in the work, than to think about all the hours that still remained. She felt her throat burn with exertion as she sucked at the smoky air.

With the path cut, they began to spray.

They had to be conservative with their water. With only the river and an inconsistent pump, wasted water was the difference between extinguishing the fire or letting it spread. They used the backpack pump, lovingly dubbed "piss cans," strapped to their backs to douse the flames. They cleared a section of every hint of fire before pressing further. Sometimes that meant dousing a tree to the roots.

It was the chill in the air that told Emma that nighttime had neared. She didn't open her mouth to tell Andrew, though, keeping quiet until he told them it was time to pack it in. They began bundling the hoses, rolling them into melons, and hiked down the trail, back to the camp they had made the night before.

There was nothing Emma wanted to do more than collapse, but she knew the second she stopped moving she would pass out and didn't want to do that in the open air. The crew began to make jokes, raw voices cracking from disuse over the day.

"We did it," Andrew told them as they assembled sandwiches for dinner. Distantly, Emma realized she'd forgotten to eat lunch in the strain of the day, but her stomach only felt like a hard knot. "There aren't any traces of that fire showing in this sector. It's dead. They can't pull us out tonight, but first thing in the morning they'll extract us."

As sleep swallowed Emma, she stepped into her other life.

***

There were hooves, tails, teeth, beaks, and more eyes on the people around her than Emma could ever count, but she didn't feel afraid. These were her people, the people of Pauvrie who had fled with her as flames licked up the trees that had been their home. They were at a safe distance now, watching the smoke pour into the sky, blackening it until it was inky dark, and yet still the smoke billowed. It hurt her heart, but what could she do? She wasn't that strange girl in her dreams who rode in helicopters and dove into the hearts of forests to combat wildfires. The most she could do was stay out of the way of the people trying to fix things.

Except there weren't any.

No wildfire had ever threatened Pauvrie or any other city in this land before in living memory; therefore, no one knew how to fight them. They fled, just as she had. They felt fear, just as strongly as she. The loss was insurmountable – these weren't just trees burning, these were homes, a city, and innumerable people had already been lost in the spreading flames. Dead, or misplaced, no one knew.

Emma huddled with a group of perhaps twenty creatures – an assortment of sapient beings like herself, but none that looked like her. They hid in a cave behind a waterfall together, protected from the flames – and the smoke – with the clarifying mist. She hugged her knees, blinking tears that rolled down her ash-streaked face.

Haino crouched down beside Emma and extended a sympathetic, feather-covered hand. Haino, who had been the reason that Emma had escaped the flames that had crept up her home while she slept. Emma still bore the red scratches on her shoulders from where Haino's claws had dug in when she had rescued Emma, and her elbows were still raw from the crash landing they had made.

"You will be okay?" Haino asked, cocking her head in a bird-like mannerism. Emma leaned her head against Haino's arm, soft blue-black feathers tickling her cheek.

"Why'd the flames come here too, Haino?" Emma asked. Haino knew about the other world – *here,* such a concept wasn't so terribly unbelievable. Emma had told her stories that sounded almost heroic when spoken out loud, yet Emma's cheeks had always gone red when telling them. "What will we do?"

Haino's head bobbed in a shrug. "We move on. We move out of the fire's way. I can take you with my people instead, or we find other oo-muns for you to live with."

Emma shook her head, even though it felt hypocritical to say it. "We can't just run away." She reached up and wiped the tears from her eyes, repeating it to herself. She had run away, and what had happened? An entire marvelous city made of trees and the weaving of a multitude of cultures and people was being destroyed, one flame-ridden tree at a time. "No, we can't run away." She felt herself growing resolute in a way she had never needed to be in this world. She drew on the strength and the memory of that other Emma, the one that had just snuffed out a small fire with her IA Crew. Sometimes this Emma thought she was dreaming of another Emma that lived far in the future or past, but either way she knew – she had knowledge no one else in this world possessed. "We can't leave Pauvrie to fall."

Haino shook her head. "Pauvrie is already gone," she said, and her beak-like lips made it sound like a coo. "It burns, flames spreading."

"But it's not gone," Emma said. Fire was not linear, but it could not consume the entire city in a single day. Not that city. The main wildfire would have destroyed it, but that one had missed the city, and only its fanning flames had approached, a smaller flank attacking the city. "We can't let Pauvrie go. It represents..." she struggled to find the words.

"It is the coming-together," Haino agreed. Pauvrie was the first place like it, and the idea of it had spawned other cities of communion. Every type of sapient and sentient creature had found a place there, living in the tree-top homes or down burrowing in the roots. Every creature had its niche. It was a cultural icon.

If it was lost, what would happen to the other cities? When they discovered that every resident had run away, back to their own communities, and not helped each other? It was about precedent.

"We have to go back."

***

The helicopter arrived at six in the morning. At the direction of Andrew, the crew Alpha, they were already packed and ready, trekking down the mountain to a clearing big enough for the helicopter to land. Already the smoke was thinner than it had been the last two days, dissipating thanks to their efforts. There were other fires, though, bigger ones further away, and so the air would not clear entirely. Still, the cleaner air felt nice to breathe. Underneath the smell of smoke, Emma could almost taste the forest, the wet dirt and green leaves.

In the helicopter Owen chatted constantly, his mouth barely pausing for him to take a breath. "We *smothered* that fire!" He said, his voice coming through the headphones they wore to protect their ears. He laughed to himself, and his positivity was infectious. Before long the rest of them were smiling as well. Even Megan, who had crossed her arms and closed her eyes, settled back to catch some more sleep while she could. "I think that's the biggest little one we stopped, and in decent timing too. I thought, after how bad the smoke was and all the embers, that we were absolutely staying out there another day."

As they lifted into the sky, Emma leaned over to look out at the window. Haze hovered in the treetops, and she remembered the other world. She turned towards Andrew.

"Hypothetically," she asked, then paused. It always took her a moment to adjust to hearing her own voice echo back to her in the headset. "If all of PG was on fire, like a big fire somehow began spreading into town, what would the first steps be to stop it?"

Andrew shrugged, his broad shoulders bumping into Owen with the movement. "Exit routes and evacuate first," he said. Emma could see the slight glaze of his eyes and knew that he was already imagining it. Andrew had a fantastic imagination, and in his downtime he apparently liked to be a DM for his DND group. "How big are the flames? How much of the city is covered?"

Emma thought for a moment. "Rank three to rank five, depending on the area. A rank five definitely rolled past, and threes are sprouting up in its wake. And at least a quarter of the city is covered. The rest... real smoky."

"Well, ranks refer to wildfires, not once they are in a city – it doesn't really work that way. I was thinking percentages." Emma felt a little bit chatisized, but she didn't interrupt. She hadn't dealt much with the in-town firefighters, so she didn't know that there were different ways to categorize fire. Fire was fire, to her. There was also the issue that Pauvrie was more like a forest fire than a regular city fire, considering the city was made of forest.

"What if it was a heavily forested city? So, still like PG, but all the streets were lined with big trees."

"That would probably make a mess of the roadwork. Big trees mean big roots."

"We've got magical roads that accommodate the roots, then."

Andrew scratched at his three-day old stubble. "Well, fire breaks are important to set up. The highways sort of act as them – ninety-seven would act as one, as it's pretty wide. But a rank five can easily jump the highway. Structural Protection Units would set up sprinklers to douse the not-yet burning sections of the city, tackle the smaller, less out-of-control fires. SPU's are manned by a combination of people, whoever is available to help – BCWS, volunteer firefighters, anyone with experience who can help. In a city, it's not one big fire – it would be a bunch of smaller burns on buildings, spreading erratically. The best set-up would be one central command centre distributing the resources and organizing all the different groups with everyone reporting back to it, but it would likely be chaotic. PG isn't high density, which may help, but I'm not sure about the building materials. Maybe take some of the grassy areas and use the drip-torches to help remove potential fuel sources." He shrugged, bumping Owen again. "A city would be more than an IA crew though. More than just one Unit Crew. You'd need huge numbers to help stop it. No matter what, there are going to be losses. When recruiting volunteers, remember: take all the help you can get."

The houses in Pauvrie are made of trees, though, Emma thought. What would that mean for the fight?

"Rank five is massive, though. Stopping one of those would mean creating fire breaks well ahead of where it's going to be. Otherwise, it is just going to roll right through anything in its path. If it hit a city dead-on, there would be no saving it."

They touched down on the ground, and as the crew stumbled out they let out collective whoops when they realized where they had arrived – an oil camp. Owen, as it was his first year, was understandably confused by the sudden excitement of the other IA members.

"Oil camps have the *best* resources," Megan told him. "Now let's go find our bunks."

As they were guided to their rooms and took a moment to shower before being deployed to the next fire, Emma kept replaying Andrew's guidance in her head.

No matter what, there are going to be losses. But how could she minimize them?

***

The first day they had tried to beat back the flames with water scooped and distributed from the waterfall in buckets, but it was a losing battle. The flames fervently fought all attempts to quell them.

On remembering the conversation she had the day before, Emma switched her focus – evacuation and egress.

In the panic of the initial spread of fire, Pauvrie had not been intentionally evacuated. Many people had run – but only a quarter of the city burned, and many of the denizens had deigned to stay despite the choking smoke. Bridges, flung between treetops, were cut and dropped with the hope of stopping the spreading flames.

Yet embers hung in the air, floating, heating more trees, finding purchase on tinder.

"If we find ourselves cut off from the waterfall and the river, we won't be able to fight and might not even be able to escape," she told the mismatched crew of about twenty she had assembled, Haino at her side. She was afraid of someone freezing in a panic when the flames came barreling forward, picked up by the wind. "We need to keep an open line of water flowing."

That was much easier with the help of the Merthen's, the people of the water. They could fill up their second lungs full of water, like water sacs, and douse the ground, saturating the earth enough to drown any possibility of flames arising. It was an effort for them to walk so far on land while essentially holding their breath, but they had help. The Guthrera, a bipedal bison-like people with large horns and huge hands, helped pull carts of the Merthens to and from the flames. At first there were only four Merthens and two Guthreras in the crew that Emma commanded, but by the end of the first day, word had spread and three more Merthens had decided to lend their lungs.

Haino worked to help evacuate those who were stuck in their tree-homes, isolated from the others through broken bridges and trapped by flames. She worked alone at her task, as all the other people of the sky had fled back to their homes at the first sign of trouble. Nevertheless, she still had the help of ravens. Like the other world, there were many ravens here, but unlike the other world, these ravens could speak. Although they were still more animal than people, they were helpful. They circled above the smoke, noting trapped citizens for Haino to rescue, and kept Emma updated on the progress of the flames.

The tips of Haino's feathers were singed as she limped along the ground and collapsed into Emma's arms at the end of the day. Emma guided Haino into the cart the Guthrera pulled and told her crew they had done enough today. They would retreat to the waterfall, recoup their strength, and get back to work tomorrow.

One raven hopped along the ground up to Emma when they were back and resting in the cave, the sound of the waterfall a soothing roar. She could barely hear the raven's squawks and had to lean close to understand the words.

"The fire moves," it told her. As it spoke, she saw visions of fire curling around sparse trees and grey-marbled rocks. Emma collapsed to her knees – the other city hadn't been warned. They had been directly in the path of the main wildfire, the same wildfire that had done so much damage to her city just by passing *near*. There had been no fire breaks. "The city on the mountains is in flames."

***

The oil camp was a welcome reprieve, but short. Emma's crew barely had time to shower, eat, sleep, shower and eat again before they were told it was time to move out. They had no time to mingle with the other people stationed there – a Unit Crew as well as a couple groups of contractors – although Emma doubted there would have been much mingling even if there had been time. It was just how things were – she stayed with her group, other people stayed with theirs.

It didn't help that she wasn't sure how to interact with the contractors when she came across them. There were fierce rivalries that she hardly understood, rivalries that had lasted longer than any firefighter's time out in the field. If they had ever been based on an actual grievance, all memory of the action was gone. Usually it only manifested as playful jeering or trash talk when they were in the same vicinity. There was also another aspect that made Emma a little uncomfortable – most of the contractor crews didn't require background checks and would apparently hire pretty much anyone, as long as they were physically able to do the work. Add in how most people preferred to stick with their own crew in case of a sudden deployment, and it made a situation where intermingling was difficult and uncommon.

Emma preferred the comfort and familiarity of her own crew. They were like family, and she trusted them more than anyone else. If something happened to her, Emma knew her crew would get her out and to safety.

The hardest part was that she knew she would see none of them next year.

Well, she might see them. If they were stationed at the same camp for a few days, or decided to visit each other while on their "weekends," as few of those as there may be. But having the same days off was unlikely, and there was something about the instant bond that formed with each new crew. At the start of each season, everyone was sorted into their IA crews for the year. The Alphas kept their same designation, but all the rest – Bravos, Charlies, and Deltas – were shuffled around to new Alphas. It was unlikely she would ever be on the same team as any of them again. Megan would be an Alpha next year, and who knew how many more years Andrew had left in him before retiring. Fire-fighting was a job for the young, and the summers bathed in smoke were brutal. None but the toughest kept on for more than a few years. Emma doubted Owen would last more than a season or two. Despite how well he seemed to keep up, she could see the resolve in him slipping with each night spent out in the woods with sticks poking into his back through the sleeping bag. Sure, she could be wrong. There was something to be said about how enticing wildfire fighting was – it was almost like an addiction, pulling people back until their bodies were wasted. But still she doubted Owen would be a long-term recruit.

Emma even doubted she would be either. It was hard to admit, but she knew that the only reason she had signed up initially was because of the strange premonition that she was *meant* to join. If she hadn't heard the name Wildlands – a name that practically was never said, now that she was in it – she doubted she ever would have signed up.

As they loaded into a truck to drive away, Emma watched out the window at the other crews and the contractors as they began to mill about and grab breakfast while chatting and laughing amiably. A pang of envy struck her when she thought about how they didn't have to get up as early, would only have to work eight or nine hours, not the likely twelve to fourteen that her crew would. How could they laugh, when two worlds burned?

***

Emma watched, rage filling her; rage she had never known in this world but had intimately experienced in the other. Rage and experience told her that if the Kyavuens were forced out, they would never be allowed back in. They would never have a chance to repair their image, mend their relationships with the other peoples of this world. This act would only perpetuate a cycle of prejudice.

Kyavuens were a people of fire. Emma did not believe they were responsible for the wildfires that threatened Pauvrie and now also Quetalien, a stone-carved city nestled in the forested mountains north of Pauvrie; and yet the mob, looking for someone to blame for the loss of their homes, had turned to the Kyavuens with hatred. The Kyavuens had not fled with the others when the flames had poured in. They were impervious to heat and the smoke did not bother them. This seemed to cast doubt on their innocence.

Emma knew it could not be true. Their flames were caused by plucking the hair from their head – or bodies – and would not alight while still attached, the act of plucking a form of ignition. As far as she could see, none of the Kyavuens were bald or lacking enough hair to instigate an aggressive fire. Yes, they were fire-starters, but not destructively so. Their fires, born of their wick-like hairs, were used in ceremonial events and helped keep the city lamps lit.

"No!" Emma shouted, her arm slicing through the charged air. She stepped in between the Kyavuens and the growing mob. "I can not – no, I will not let you do this. These people are not our enemies." She shook her head – nobody understood. She remembered last year in the other world, when she'd had to go door to door to tell people they needed to evacuate from a small town that was being consumed by wildfire. Dry grass had caught fire and the wind had blown – hardly more than a puff, and yet an entire field had turned into a blaze in minutes. The people she had warned had fought her, argued, rolled their eyes. "I'm not leaving my home!" They told her. She couldn't force them, only warn them. "You just set the fire on purpose to force us out of here!" they accused, with wobbling fingers and bared teeth. Those people didn't understand that yes, sometimes BCWS and the contractors used their drip torches to burn fuel – but that was to starve the bigger fires, stop them from spreading, deprive them of the kindling they needed to expand. But they only saw firefighters lighting fires, and so they fought against what they believed was the forced false evacuations.

Now various citizens of Pauvrie sought to expel their believed malefactors.

"The Kyavuens are not your enemy," she repeated. "And neither is fire." An idea was forming, something she was annoyed hadn't come to her sooner. She turned to the Kyavuens, setting her mouth in a determined grimace as she surveyed the group. "I know how you can help." She pointed to the brush that littered the forest floor, ages of abandoned refuse that had grown in heaps underneath the forest-top city, perfect fuel for the wind-blown sparks. "A fire cannot burn if it is starved. Today, we will make fire breaks."

***

Her two lives ran in parallel to each other. Where once she was provided respite from the flames in Wildlands, she now fought them in both. Smoke burned her lungs in both worlds. Her eyes wept red. But she continued fighting, continued working, continued pushing herself to the limits.

In BC, her IA crew was dropped from fire to fire, stopping the spread of small flames that bloomed under the August sun. Some fires took days to put out; sometimes they put out multiple fires in a day.

In Wildlands she worked with the growing population of refugees who were determined to get their homes back. Pauvrie was broken and burnt, but it was not utterly destroyed, and so the hope that they could rebuild the city that sat on top of the forest remained. With the help of the Kyavuen's burning the garbage and dead plant life that had accumulated under the city, the fires found less hospitable purchase on the forest floor. With the help of the Merthen's drenching the soil, flames that burned in roots were stifled.

Emma taught the people of Wildlands about LACES – Lookouts, Anchor Points, Communications, Escape Routes, and Safety Zones – and began organizing the growing number of volunteers around that. The Ravens flying overhead were fantastic lookouts, black wings streaking shadows against the grey, ash-filled sky.

Emma reached out, letting ash land in her hand like snowflakes.

***

They were back in an oil camp for the day, and Emma slumped over her breakfast, poking at runny eggs with her fork. She should have been ravenous – she *was* ravenous – but she was dually exhausted. The past week had been the hardest of both her lives.

They'd lost another section of Pauvrie, and the fires were scorching the stone streets of Quetalien. The marble pillars and statues that lined the city streets cracked as the wildfire leapt from gardens and trees. Emma could only do so much for the second city, so far from her own. There just weren't enough people, no matter how freely she shared the resources and knowledge she held.

And here, they'd lost another ten thousand hectares to a fire that seemed to bloom fiercer with every drop of water they gave it. There was talk among the crews that this one was going to rival the fire of Battleship Mountain. Every hot, windy day was foreboding, and the small town this fire was near had already been evacuated. Her team had been bounced around, putting out the small fires that kept sprouting under the heat dome, crushing whirling micro-tornadoes of flame before they could gain a foothold. Emma was sure that she would never be able to fully scrub the ash from her skin.

Emma heard a squawk and looked up, narrowing her eyes at the sky. "What'd he say?" she mumbled, only loud enough for Andrew to hear before catching herself, remembering she was in the wrong world, where ravens did not give her information about the spread of wildfires.

Andrew had followed her gaze, catching the corvid looping lazy circles near the edge of the camp. "Probably saying 'throw me a bite of those half-cooked eggs,'" Andrew joked, eyeing up his own plate warily.

Owen and Megan were having a spirited conversation about whether one of the men at an adjacent table – a contractor – had been giving either of them the eye. They both seemed to agree that the man – broad-shouldered with dark eyes and enviously long lashes – had winked at one of them. Unfortunately, they could not seem to agree.

"He looks straighter than an arrow!" Megan insisted with a hiss, jerking her head.

"Hey, arrows wobble when they fly," insisted Owen.

"They spin, too," Andrew added, turning away from Emma. "Discovered that in a campaign I was running. Yes, the angle of the arrowhead *did* matter."

Megan chuckled. "And how much do *you* wobble?" she asked Owen.

In response, he gave a full-body wiggle.

The group laughed, and Emma gave a weak smile. Andrew met her eyes with a softness that seemed almost fatherly, despite only being a few years older than her. "You okay?" he asked, bumping his shoulder against hers.

Emma opened her mouth to speak, but suddenly a brown-haired, lightly stubbled guy of about twenty years old dropped down into the seat across from her. "Mind if I sit here?" he asked, but began forking eggs into his mouth before anyone could answer. "So, who are you under? I don't think I've seen you in the group yet. Just get in?"

"Yeah, actually," Andrew said. Emma stayed silent, exchanging a glance with Megan and Owen. They all felt the tension. "We are IA."

"Oh!" He seemed almost happy about it. "I've heard about you all, diving into the smaller fires in little groups. It seems so cool, but I'm okay with staying back a little further. I'm only doing this for the first time – thought I'd make a few extra bucks over summer for school. I'm Luke, by the way." He lifted a hand and held it out over the table, and it hovered awkwardly in the air for a moment as everyone on Emma's crew stared at it. Luke froze, hand still hanging in the air. "Oh... you aren't... elitist about it, are you? I've heard some things from the other members of my crew, but I thought that they were just exaggerating..."

Andrew reached his hand out and shook Luke's still-outstretched palm. "No," he said firmly, then withdrew his hand, a smile on his face. "Welcome to wildfire fighting. We can always take all the help we can get. Now, we were having a very important conversation – who do you think that guy over there would have been winking at? Megan and Owen here are sure he was flirting with one of them, but see, I think they are neglecting a very likely third candidate – *me.*"

***

Haino descended from the skies in a heap of feathers at Emma's feet. "They are coming," she said, wheezing. She turned away to cough and Emma stretched out a supportive hand, gently rubbing circles on Haino's back, careful to not ruffle her feathers.

"Who?" she asked when the coughs subsided. They were all coughing – all had been for days. It wasn't just the fire that burned in both worlds – her lungs did too. The air was too thick to breathe, but they still pushed forward.

In response Haino lifted a winged arm, pointing.

Emma could see a crowd crawling towards her, uneven gaits rolling forward. She felt the hair on her arms rise. It was late, she should be sleeping, but she had clung to this world for just a little longer, hoping to hold Haino in her arms before she slept. Now it seemed that there was trouble awaiting her, and bed would not come yet. Exhaustion sagged her shoulders.

The mismatched crowd assembled before Emma.

"We'd like to help," said one of the people of the night with curling horns and yellow fangs, and one of the people from the underground with pale skin and too-large eyes agreed.

They were numerous – Klotolrs, Jphentos, Diachetars, Lufingyas, and other peoples that Emma could not remember the names of – and they all offered their help. Yet the group terrified Emma. She did not know these people, and they could only vouch for each other. Some of these people could be monsters that skulked underground or in the city at night. They could be anything, evil or just misunderstood; she did not know. To work beside any of them could even mean working beside someone who ate nightmares. She'd heard the stories growing up, just like any child of Pauvrie.

Or they could be what she needed.

She looked out at the assembled crowd of inhuman faces, with terrifying teeth and twisted features, and realized that they were not so different than the crowd that she had sat with in the cave that first day. These people were threatened by the flames too. More light would touch the forest floor if the fires were left to burn everything to a crisp. These denizens would be disturbed – the ones that could not see in strong light would be blinded by it, and the ones that could be hurt by sunlight would die from it come winter. Their habitat would be lost, and unlike many of the others who, while displaced, could easily find a new niche elsewhere, these people would struggle to relocate. Even the burrowers were at risk, their dens filling with ash.

There was only one solution.

"Tell me how you would like to help."

***

Emma emptied the last of her piss can onto the tree in front of her. The flame had already been extinguished, but when she placed a hand onto the bark, she could still feel the heat that burned underneath, ready to flare again. She felt a prickle of frustrated tears at the corner of her eyes. They'd been out here for two days, putting out tiny fires that just kept sprouting. It was terrifying – no matter how careful they were with drenching the area and extinguishing the fires, it felt as if the trees themselves harboured the flames, ready to alight again as soon as the crew blinked or dared to turn away. The heat was excruciating; the sun, even behind the smoke, was menacing.

And her cough had grown worse.

It wasn't uncommon to cough. They worked out in the smoke, day-in and day-out, inhaling the worst the world had to offer. With each gasping breath Emma felt her lungs age another month, and wondered how many packs of cigarettes a day she was inhaling the equivalent of. She wondered how long the waiting list was for lung transplants.

"Let's call it," Andrew called out to the crew. "Wrap 'em up and bring the melon's back to the truck. I've already disconnected the pump." Emma felt a flash of irritation – of course she knew the hose had already turned off, she could see the drip of the last dregs of water escaping. And she could also see that they were almost done, that maybe half an hour more and they'd have neutralized the fire.

"We should keep going," she said, even though she had to blink the tears out of her eyes to say it. She felt them run down her cheeks, no doubt cutting trails through the ash that powdered her skin. "We're almost done the section, if we leave it –"

Andrew shot her a sharp look. She could see how red his eyes were. His lips were pinched together and his nostrils flared – whether in annoyance or trying to suck in air, she could not tell. "We're done for the day. We aren't getting this cleared out tonight."

Emma felt a surge of anger. "We *can* get it cleared, if we just –"

"We're *not*," He repeated firmly. "Bravo, Delta, get wrapping and head to the truck." Megan and Owen ducked their heads in agreement and turned around stiffly, wrapping their hoses. Andrew waited until they were almost out of earshot and then turned to Emma. "What the hell do you think you're doing, Charlie?"

Her designation felt like a slap to the face. Emma blinked for a moment, staring up at Andrew. The sudden bout of anger she felt seemed to flare out as quickly as it had come.

It hurt, but he was right. In this world she was just a Charlie, just third in the pecking order of a four-person crew. The only person she could possibly hope to boss around and not get in trouble for it was Owen. What had she been thinking?

It had been the other world leaking through, she knew. She'd been handing out commands left and right, pushing everyone – herself included – just a little harder, just a little farther. They'd made great strides in Pauvrie – the city had almost been reclaimed from the fires. With the renewed help from the people of the underground and the night, they'd been able to double the hours they were fighting fires – no longer fighting fire by daylight, but by moonlight too. Sometimes they could even see the halo of the moon through the smoke.

But people had been collapsing from exhaustion. Each day they lost a couple more, people who had to be sent far away to be treated. People who pushed themselves as hard as they could, coughing violently, until they could not take another step.

"I'm sorry," Emma sobbed, feeling the exhaustion rushing up to crush her. "I just want it to be over."

***

Quetalien, once beautiful, was now rubble. At the insistence of Haino, Emma had left Pauvrie on the back of an eagle-headed, bat-winged person named Kohten. Haino flew beside them, gliding effortlessly through the evening air. Up here the smoke was thinner, but so was the air, and Emma felt faint. Clinging perhaps a bit too tight, she was terrified of fainting and then accidentally pitching herself over the side. The sight of Quetalien in ruins felt like a shot of caffeine in her veins.

"It's gone," she whispered to the air, even though it wasn't true. The city still stood – the stone-carved buildings were mostly fine, if stripped of all the wood and rug decorations that had previously adorned them – but the fantastical carvings that had lined the streets and city entrances were crumbled, shattered against the ground.

Kohten touched down on the ground ungainly, and Emma slid off his back. He was a giant, and so she felt as if she were free-falling for a couple feet before she landed against the hard ground. Black, soot-scorched stone paths marked the way into the city, and Emma walked forward hesitantly. Her footsteps echoed eerily in the empty streets.

There wasn't much for Emma to survey. She wasn't an architect in any life that she knew of, and she had no idea of the structural integrity of the fire-washed buildings. She kept out in the open, not daring to duck into doorways no matter how curious she was. Instead, she walked through the silent streets, her soft boots pressing into the ash like it was freshly fallen snow.

Emma returned to the entrance half an hour later, where Haino and Kohten still waited. "We'll send in the ash-eaters," she told them. It was all she could do for the city.

***

The ash-eaters, as they were dubbed, worked to clear the debris left behind from the wildfires. Previously a people of the underground used to create fertilizer from refuse, some of them had discovered that they had quite an appetite for ash. Transported to Quetalien, they immediately got to work clearing the city.

Emma didn't know when it would be safe for people to come back. She didn't want to amend "if ever" after that thought, but sometimes it came unbidden. It was as she had feared – many of the stone-work buildings began to topple once disturbed. Clearing the debris was slow, dangerous work.

She didn't like what it meant for Pauvrie. Emma wondered if she would ever see her home restored to its former glory. When her thoughts grew dark, sometimes she wondered if it had been worth battling back the wildfires at all. Perhaps they should have just moved on, let the fires consume, set up somewhere safer.

It was a tantalizingly nihilistic thought, she knew. But her work in both worlds told her the full story. Yes, they could move on – maybe they even should have. But duty compelled her to try and at least redirect the fires where they could, extinguish them where they should. Sometimes it made sense to move away from the fire, but Pauvrie shouldn't have burned. Quetalien shouldn't have either; they should have been prepared. Perhaps then the devastation could have lessened.

Emma felt ready to relinquish command. The truth was that she had been ready weeks ago, if not earlier. She didn't know the right thing to do – she'd only been trying what she thought needed to be done, but seeing the devastation in Quetalien and the slow progress in Pauvrie made her doubt herself. And there was an ache in her chest as she thought about how many she had pushed to exhaustion in her quest to try and save the city. It had been futile – but it also hadn't. They were down to the smallest flames, but so much of the city had burned that it was no longer recognizable. When could anyone move back? The falling buildings in Quetalien bode ill for the tree-formed homes, blackened and brittle, of Pauvrie.

But then, one day, the last of the fires in Pauvrie went out.

Smoke still blanketed the skies but Emma knew with a few big gusts they too would blow away. Ravens circled overhead, and their caws spoke of hope. She dismissed them and they fanned out, no doubt to chase the winds and see where the fire still crawled. Emma knew that somewhere fire would continue to burn; it was the cycle of things, the nature of it all. But at least Pauvrie was now safe.

Emma climbed with aching limbs and then stood on the remains of the tree-topped city. In the distance she could see swaying brush, but much closer were the blackened husks of what remained. Far below she could see people at work, cleaning, sorting, and regrowing. The soil, rejuvenated by the ash processed by the ash-eaters, was already proving to be nutritious to the sprouting seedlings. There was talk of new growth, of new opportunities to rebuild. But it would take time. People had to come back, and as it was right now, most would be too afraid. Even though the flames were gone, the heat and the memory of the fire would remain.

***

Emma choked on the smoke and found she could not catch her breath.

The day rushed by her in snatches. Collapsing on the trail. Megan and Andrew pulling her out of the bush, loading her into the truck. Pine needles scraping against the window as Andrew drove, Owen sitting beside her, his soot-covered face filled with worry. The beat of wind off of helicopter blades stirring her hair. The hiss of a mask placed over her face.

And then darkness, for longer than she knew. Darkness that did not take her to the other world.

When she woke she did not know how long it had been and refused to ask. Nurses stopped by her bedside. The monitors beeped intermittently. There was a rushing sound in her ears that wouldn't quiet. Sometimes she was wracked with coughs for a minute straight, until her stomach seized and her eyes watered. Her throat ached, but the oxygen mask strapped against her face prevented her from taking a single sip of water. She watched the drip-drip-drip of the IV bag beside her.

Sleep eluded Emma; she was terrified to slip into its soft embrace, terrified of the yawning black that would greet her on the other side. If she was meant to save Wildlands, if that had been her whole purpose, then clearly her job was done and now she would never be allowed to return. The thought was harrowing. She sobbed between coughs. When a nurse saw her tear-streaked face, she told Emma, "Your crew is doing okay. Don't you worry about them. You just get better now. Everything is going to be okay." Emma turned away to face the wall in response, feeling guilty that she had barely thought about her IA crew in the intervening hours of wakefulness. Now she wondered – were they on standby until she was out of the hospital? IA crews were strictly managed and didn't operate one down – they only operated in crews of three when there were no Deltas in the squad.

A painful ache formed in her chest, and she realized that she missed them. Even when they were on days off they were always in close contact with one another. Being on-call meant being at the dispatch area together within thirty minutes. Emma had no idea where her crew members were, nor which hospital she was at. The square of her window showed smoky sky, but no tell-tale signs of what city she was in. She wanted to grab her phone and see if anyone had tried to get a hold of her, but she didn't know where it was. Besides, she could feel a heaviness settle over her body. She wasn't sure if she could lift her arms to search.

In that moment Emma realized that, despite the pain she felt with each breath, she would trade anything to be back out there with her crew. The memory of the backpack pump straps dug into her shoulders as if she were still standing out in the forest. She could picture the faces of her IA crew with painstaking clarity.

Emma closed her eyes and slowed her breathing, finally letting sleep overtake her.

When she opened her eyes, she saw a cluster of blue-black feathers and the tilt of beak-like lips, slightly parted, beside her. Emma slowly sat up, holding her breath, afraid to disturb the dream and dispel it.

Haino stirred awake; her beautiful, deep brown eyes fluttered open and then gazed lovingly at Emma. Emma swallowed hard. "I'm still here," she said, her voice a croak.

"Of course you are," Haino cooed. She ruffled her feathers and then pulled herself into a sitting position beside Emma. Their knees touched, and the feathers tickled at Emma's skin. "The Vallco kin reached out to my people, and they have more friends they can send our way. They are people of the sky as well, but they are very strong, very large, able to carry heavy weights in their talons." She swept one wing towards her own, weaker, claws as if to demonstrate their frailty in comparison. Emma thought to protest – it was those same claws that had, although pierced her, also saved her life when her home was burning. But she knew that Haino only meant to highlight the benefits of welcoming these new people to the cause.

Emma hugged her knees to her chest for a moment, grounding herself. She was really here, she realized. The dream hadn't ended. She paused for a moment, wondering if the dream would perhaps end here instead. Would she never visit that other world ever again? Was it cut off to her now? It was the same thought she had in the other world, only reflected.

She sighed deeply and then stood, offering a hand to pull Haino to her feet – claws – as well. She held onto Haino's hand.

The fires had been put out in Pauvrie, but there were other cities that could be at risk, other sites that would need to be managed. They could run, or they could help the fire pass with minimal loss. Emma knew that no matter the choice, she would be there to help.

She thought of that other her, nearly comatose in the hospital bed, sucking in oxygen and breathing out tears, uncertain of her future. Emma knew exactly what that other her would do.

"Tell them to come," Emma said. "We need all the help we can get."

ACKNOWLEDGEMENTS

As we close out this anthology, I'd like to give my appreciation to the many people who helped make this a possibility. Without all of your love, support, and interest, this project may have never made it past the idea stage and would not have become the collection it is today.

First of all, I'd like to thank my fellow writers and friends, who doubled as beta-readers, let me bounce ideas off them, and helped decide on the fifty million iterations of covers and other design elements I put together. I apologize for any wasted writing time due to being a chatterbox and I hope to keep seeing you all at future writing events!

A huge thank you to all the authors in this anthology! Without your stories and poems, this project wouldn't have been possible. I would love to work with all of you again on any future projects, and I feel so fortunate to have been able to put this together with your help.

Next, I want to send a huge thank you to all our Kickstarter backers who helped support this anthology: Cecilia Castro, Rachel Preston, Russell Smith, Shirley Moore, Kristen Altmann, Deb Robertson & Alan Preston, J Fischer, and everyone else who backed the project!

Thank you Kilmeny MacMichael for being my secondary editor for all the poetry, and always being available for me to float ideas. You helped catch details I didn't and helped narrow down what was working. I loved being able to try so many different things with you – you were a great tester for all the parts of the project. I hope to work with you on all sorts of other adventures in the future! Also, I really hope to have an in-person write-in with you one day!

Lindi Ammundsen, thank you for so many different things! You were an amazing resource for all things fire-fighting – from the first conversations when the initial sparks of "All The Help We Can Get" ignited; to helping find places to host our write-ins and joining me on them so often and being a great writing buddy; to tolerating my incessant chattiness during our write-ins; to answering even more of my questions when they popped up; and finally, for reading (and re-reading) the final iteration of the story until we were sure we got the details somewhere within the realm of accurate.

Thank you, Jen Herkes, for your eloquent interview. If you ever want to grab a coffee, get comfy on those chairs, and tell me another story, I will gladly take you up on it.

Dael King-Smith, I appreciate your candidness when talking about your experiences in Wildfire Fighting. You provided so much personal insight, and I'm grateful for all the work you do and the help you've provided answering my ongoing questions.

Thank you, Tyree Corfe, for helping me understand all the different roles various groups fulfill in Wildfire services. I appreciated the clarity and candor in your interview, and I'm glad I was able to have the time to sit down and talk with you about it all.

Graham Pearce, you helped me sharpen the fine edges of my stories and illuminate what exactly makes a story shine. You helped me become more confident in this writing journey. I appreciate your unwavering willingness to look over my work, even before we'd ever actually met. I hope to have many more stories to send your way in the future.

Thank you, Topper Sundquist, for beta-reading "Flax Finds a Flameling." I'm sorry I made you read "creature" so many times, and I promise I axed at least fifty percent of them in the final rendition.

Danuta Gigliotti, thank you so much for helping me hone my poetry. Your open, approachable demeanour reassured me that I could share my poems with you, and your effective teaching style helped me understand much more about what makes poetry compelling.

And to my husband, Jordan. Thank you for all the support you gave me as I worked on this project, and all the years before that you've been a steadfast advocate for my writing. I appreciate all the naps and nights you took over for our daughter so that I could squeeze in an extra half hour of editing or two hours of writing these past few months. I promise to not be so busy again until July, when my next project is in full swing.

BIOGRAPHIES

Studying Romantic literature and eco-poetry, **Raegan Cote** is a first year English Master's student at the University of Northern British Columbia. She was born in Prince George, BC and has always had an adoration for this Northern city. Raegan has been published in Pulp Mill Fiction Vol. 1 and Vol. 2. She aspires to be a teacher one day.

Tyree Corfe is a poet living in Prince George, BC. They recently graduated from the University of Northern BC and are currently pursuing a career in the performing arts. Tyree has also worked as a wildland firefighter in 2021 drawing literary inspiration from the experience. They have been published in Pulpmill Fiction Volume 1 and 2 and are currently writing a poetry book inspired by their time firefighting.

Asha Jade Goodwin is an author of Science Fiction and Fantasy stories. She loves books that leave the reader questioning the ending and will always enjoy a good tragedy. She is a Canadian writer as well as an adoptee. Found family, diversity, and inclusion are important themes in her writing. Asha has been published in Triangulation: Seven-Day Weekend.

Morgan Allie Graylin is a lifelong writer from Ontario, Canada. First published at the age of thirteen, she's now reconnecting and rediscovering her love of the written word in her thirties with her debut fantasy romance novel that's set to release in 2024.

Cherie Hanson has earned: a B.A. in English; a B.Ed.; an MA in Contemporary American Poetry from UBC, Vancouver. She has written plays, musicals, non-fiction, fiction, a children's book commissioned by the Canadian Asthma Society and poetry. Her writing has been published in Canadian Women's Studies; Canadian Dimension Magazine; Cosmic Trend Magazine; Love Poems for the Media Age, Ripple Effect Press Anthology; Erasure Anthology published by Naropa University; Warrior Poets Anthology; The Pine Beetle Review; The Wine Country Writer's Anthology and in the Black Mountain Press Her Words magazine.

Payne Haynes is an author and general crazy person. They write a range of literary, science fiction, urban fantasy, and everything in between. Actively taking advantage of life in this world and so many others, they follow the stories of people who face hardships and challenges, preferring to read about regular people, hardworking people, and those who struggle to survive and face the challenges that come their way. By day Payne Haynes is an accountant, mom, and crafter; by night, a prolific writer of worlds filled with intrigue, adventure, and strife. More is always coming from the mind of Payne Haynes.

Lesley Hebert lives on the Pacific raincoast with a sociable husband and anti-social cat. Her work has appeared in Beyond Words, Canadian Stories, The First Line, Pocket Lint, A Poetry of Place: Journeys Across New Westminster and Parabola. She won first place (non-fiction) in the RCLAS 2023 writing competition.

Drea Laj calls Vancouver Island her home, after earning her undergraduate degrees in English and Education here. As an English teacher, she's nurtured young writers to reach their dreams. Now it's her turn.

Heather Bonin MacIntosh writes flash fiction that can be found in Humber Literary Review, Lavalamp, Write Word, and anthologies Blood is Thicker, and Very Much Alive. Based in Calgary, Heather likes to garden, travel to places tourists don't go, ski, and binge watch astronaut movies. She is currently editing her first novel.

Kilmeny MacMichael lives in a small town in the Okanagan Valley, where she writes flash, short fiction and the occasional poem. The first summer after she moved here from the big city back east, there was a fire on the mountain five minutes from her house. It made an impression!

Em Van Moore is a speculative fiction, science fantasy and horror writer from northern B.C. At her day job she is a hospice nurse, and at night she uses her first-hand knowledge to inspire her novels and short stories. When Em isn't working, writing or beta reading, she's spending time with her human and fur babies, or trying to befriend crows.

Cassidy Muir is a graduate student at the University of Northern British Columbia's Prince George campus. She is currently pursuing her Master's degree in English, with a creative writing focus.

Rod Raglin is a Canadian journalist, photographer and self-published author of 13 novels, two plays and a collection of short stories. He lives in Vancouver, BC, where he is the publisher and editor of an online community newspaper and a paid facilitator of creative writing circles. His short fiction and poetry has been published in several online magazines as well as being aired nationally on CBC radio. He's been a prize winner in Vancouver West End Writers' Poetry Competition.

Jonathan Riggs is an author of Fantasy, Sci-Fi, and Horror. He found a passion for writing at a young age and has been pursuing a B.A. in English. He lives in British Columbia with his wife and daughter.

Alexander Robertson is an Australian-Canadian writer, artist and designer. He loves speculative fiction, skiing and mountain biking. Born in rural Australia, he immigrated to Canada in 2017. He currently lives in Whistler, BC with his partner.

Michele Rule is a disabled writer and poet from Kelowna BC. She is published in Spillwords, Okay Donkey, Five Minute Lit, and Chicken Soup for the Soul, among others. Michele lives in a beautiful garden surrounded by people who love her just the way she is. You can find Michele at www.linktr.ee/MicheleRule.

Jaki Sawyer has always loved poetry. After living in northern Alberta until she was 39, Jaki moved to New Hampshire then retired to Kelowna, British Columbia. Jaki is published in Tiny Seed, Words for the Earth and has taken second and first place in Word on the Lake.

A Bread Loaf Scholar and Pushcart Prize nominee with an MFA in Creative Writing, **Anneliese Schultz** was shortlisted for the 2016 HarperCollins/UBC Prize for Best New Fiction. Her fiction has won numerous awards, and her stories and poetry are widely published. Anneliese works on climate fiction, Middle Grade stories, and adult literary fiction in a wildly creative German-Punjabi household in Vancouver.

Hilma Sinkinson is a 70 year old writer who discovered NaNoWriMo in 2014. With her first completed novel in 2019, Hilma started two other novels. She wants to share her knowledge of life with other women struggling to stay true to themselves. Hilma writes for that woman.

Topper Sundquist grew up in Kamloops and now lives in Prince George. He finds constant inspiration from his three kids, his brilliant wife, and how much he hates having to work a day job. He is sometimes mistaken for a sasquatch.

Lily Autumn West hails from Vancouver BC. A UBC graduate, she has been told that her stories make readers laugh hard or cry hard, with little in between. Lily mostly writes satirical fantasy and haunting prose or poetry. She drinks more tea than she reasonably should.

www.ingramcontent.com/pod-product-compliance
Lightning Source LLC
Chambersburg PA
CBHW061652190726
48289CB00006B/1847